Maya's Divided World

by
GLORIA VELÁSQUEZ

Piñata Books
Houston, Texas
1995

This book is made possible through a grant from the National Endowment for the Arts (a federal agency), the Lila Wallace-Reader's Digest Fund and the Andrew W. Mellon Foundation.

Piñata Books
An imprint of Arte Público Press
University of Houston
452 Cullen Performance Hall
Houston, Texas 77204-2004

Piñata Books are full of surprises!

Cover illustration and design by Vega Design Group

∞ The paper used in this publication meets the requirements of the American National Standard for Permanence of Paper for Printed Library Materials Z39.48-1984.

2 3 4 5 6 7 8 9 0 1   12 11 10 9 8 7 6 5 4

*For Brandi, Rena, Kelly, Dalana
and Estela, the girls from the Class of 1990*

OTHER BOOKS IN
The Roosevelt High School Series

Juanita Fights the School Board

Tommy Stands Alone

Rina's Family Secret

Maya's Divided World

ONE
Maya

I hear the door open, but I pretend that I am asleep.

"Maya, it's time to get up or you'll be late for the bus. Maya, wake up," Mom orders. "You don't want to be late on your first day of school, do you?"

This time I decide to answer her because if I don't, she'll never leave the room. I roll over on my left side so that she can see my face. Mom is standing a few feet away from me wearing one of her professor outfits. Boring and plain. "I'm already awake, Mom," I answer sarcastically.

"I have a faculty meeting this morning so I have to get going. But I'll see you after school. Call me at my office when you get home, okay, *m'ija*? Oh, I almost forgot. Juanita called. She said to tell you she'd meet you by the lockers."

I pretend not to care as Mom reaches down and gives me a light kiss on the cheek. Then she's gone and I'm left all to myself again. Lately, it seems like I'm always alone. Ever since Dad left, things have been different. Even my mom looks different. She has giant bags under her eyes. I always used to think she was pretty, but now she looks like a witch. Maybe she deserves to look that way. It's

all her fault, anyway. If she'd only paid more attention to Dad, like Grandma said, maybe we'd all still
be together.

I think back to my summer in New Mexico. It
was the worst summer vacation of my life. We had
gone to stay at Grandma's in Santa Fe for a month.
When Grandma met us at the airport, I could tell
she suspected something strange was going on
because she kept asking why Dad hadn't come with
us. Mom made up an excuse, but I could tell
Grandma didn't believe her. I don't know why Mom
lied. I guess she was afraid.

The next evening, while I was in the bedroom
playing video games, I overheard Mom talking
with Grandma.

"Mom, there's something I need to tell you. I
know it's going to be hard on you, but you have to
try to understand."

I quickly turned up the volume on the television set so they would think I couldn't hear them.
Then I went over to the doorway and sat on the
floor to listen to them. The door was barely open,
but I could still make out Grandma's face. I heard
her say, "*Madre de Dios, hija*, what is it?"

Then, I heard my mother answer her in a
shaky voice, "Armando and I have decided to
divorce."

There was a moment of silence before
Grandma finally spoke again. "*¿Estás loca?*" she
shouted. "You can't do that! It's against the church,
against God." I noticed that Grandma's face had
become deathly pale.

"I'm sorry, Mom, but that's the way it is. We've
already filed."

Grandma's voice suddenly grew louder. "I knew that this would happen sooner or later when you both went to live in California."

"Mom, it has nothing to do with that."

"*¡Cómo que no!*" Grandma protested. "The minute you left Santa Fe you started to change, going to college, paying more attention to books than to your own husband." There were tears in Grandma's eyes now and her body was slumped down in the armchair.

"Oh, Mom, you know that's not true," Mom said in a defeated voice.

"Just look at all your friends here, Sonia. They're happy being married and having kids. Why can't you be more like them?"

There was a long, awkward pause before I heard Mom answer Grandma in a weary tone I'd never heard her use before. "Mom, going to college has nothing to do with this. It's just that, well, Armando and I have grown apart for some time now. We're not the same people anymore."

"It's you, Sonia! You're the one to blame," Grandma said sharply. "If you had behaved more like a married woman."

"No, that's not true, Mom. You have to try to understand. Look at all my aunts. You're always saying how miserable their marriages are, that they all should have gotten a divorce years ago. Do you want me to end up like them?"

Grandma was yelling now. "I don't care about them. I care about you and *m'ija*. Anyway, the Church doesn't allow divorces. I'm so ashamed. What am I going to tell the family?"

"Tell them the truth, Mom."

"No, Sonia. I won't let you disgrace us. I want you to leave my home now. I don't want a *sinvergüenza* in my home. *M'ija* can stay here, but not you."

Then I saw Grandma get up and walk out of the room crying.

The next thing I heard were my mother's sobs. I wanted to run to her side and put my arms around her, but I couldn't. I sat there frozen, tears streaming down my face.

The next morning we repacked our bags and went to stay at *Tía* Lola's house. Grandma begged me to stay with her, but I told her that I had to go wherever Mom went.

During the weeks that followed, *Tía* Lola tried to get Grandma to be reasonable and talk to Mom, but it was useless. Grandma was old and stubborn. We ended up staying away from Grandma's house and avoiding family gatherings. For the first time in my life, I started to hate New Mexico. I hated everything about it, and I was glad when it came time to go home. At the airport, Mom cried more than usual when it was time to say goodbye. I knew that it was because Grandma hadn't said goodbye to us. *Tía* Lola explained to my mom that Grandma thought divorce only happened to *gringos*. She said that in time, Grandma would adjust to the idea. When we arrived back home in Laguna, I felt like my entire summer had been ruined and I started spending more time in my room.

Now that summer is over, the house seems emptier than before I went to Santa Fe and I feel lonelier than ever. I start to feel the tears coming, but it's getting late, so I force myself out of bed, determined not to let myself cry again. In the shower, I turn the water on as hot as I can stand and let it fall soothingly all over my body. I dread going to school this morning. It's hard to feel excited about being a junior at Roosevelt this year. I can't imagine what I'm going to tell my friends. I feel so ashamed. I've been avoiding calling Juanita and Rina. Maybe they won't find out about my dad. Maybe I can pretend that everything is the same as before.

When I get out of the shower, I stare at the new clothes my mom bought me in Santa Fe. I feel my eyes start to get watery. Why is it that I cry for any little thing now?

✎ ✐ ✑

I make it to the bus stop exactly as the school bus pulls up. Almost all the seats are taken and I end up having to sit next to some nerdy guys who look like freshman. Ankiza is not on the bus this morning, and I wonder if her dad drove her to school. I think about last year and my first day at Roosevelt High. Dad was so excited, he drove me to school. On the way over, we stopped for doughnuts and Dad made a joke about how he should have been a cop instead of an engineer, since he loved doughnuts so much. We both laughed so much.

I really miss Dad. If he were here now, I know I wouldn't be sitting on this stupid bus on my first day of school, listening to these dumb freshmen. I can't stand them. They act like dummies. I'm sure glad I'm a junior.

TWO
Maya

When I get to my locker, Juanita and Rina are already there waiting for me. Juanita races up to me and gives me a giant hug.

"Maya, I'm so glad to see you!" she tells me. "Your hair really got long over the summer."

I can't believe Juanita likes my hair. It's long and stringy and the color is a dirty brown, while hers is jet black, thick and wavy. "Hi. I missed you, too," I answer, trying not to sound depressed. "And you're still a *chaparrita* !" Juanita's face breaks into a big smile, revealing two large dimples. I suddenly realize how much I've missed talking with her. Juanita has been my best friend since I first came to Roosevelt. And last year, when the School Board kicked Juanita out of school for fighting, I was the one who stuck by her, helping her until the school administration finally reinstated her.

"Hey, Maya," Rina says, interrupting my thoughts. "You got any classes with me this year?"

"I'm not sure," I tell her, pulling out my schedule card. We huddle together so we can compare our schedules, and Juanita squeals with joy when she finds out we have first-period English class together. I can tell Rina is jealous, but she feels better when she notices that we have two classes together in the afternoon. Rina is my second-best friend—although sometimes she gets on my nerves because she likes to pick on all the guys.

The first bell rings, so Juanita and I quickly say bye to Rina and hurry down the hall to Mrs. Rafter's room. Everyone calls Mrs. Rafter the "Colonel" because she's the strictest teacher at Roosevelt. She's been teaching here for about thirty years. That explains why she looks so ancient.

Mrs. Rafter spends the first fifteen minutes seating us according to her new seating chart. I end up in the back of the classroom in row six, and poor Juanita gets stuck right up front. Then Mrs. Rafter orders us to take out pencil and paper and write a short composition about how we spent our summer vacation. I take out a sheet of paper and stare at it for the longest time. When I look around, I notice everyone is busy writing. My eyes start to fill with tears, but I hurry and blink them back. Finally, I decide to make up a story about how Dad, Mom and I spent the summer camping in New Mexico. I describe in detail how we spent hours hiking in the Sandía Mountains. After a while, I find myself believing it all and I start to feel better.

At lunchtime, Juanita and I head for our old spot near the football field to meet Rina and the rest of our friends. There aren't many Chicanos and African-Americans at Roosevelt, so we all hang out with each other. Ankiza and Tyrone are African-American and Rina is Puerto Rican. But Tommy and Rudy are Chicanos. When we first started hanging out together at school, all the other kids used to stare at us, but now I guess they're used to it.

When we get to the football field, Tommy, Rudy, and Tyrone are all standing next to the bleachers. They whistle at us as we sit down on the grass next to Rina and Ankiza. Tyrone keeps staring at me, but I pretend not to notice. I've been avoiding talking with him since the beginning of summer. I know he's wondering why I haven't returned his phone calls.

Tommy is the first to speak to me. "Hey, Maya. We heard you went to New Mexico? How was it?"

Now everyone's looking at me. I know I have to make something up. I can't possibly tell them the truth. "It was okay," I shrug.

"Just okay!" yells big-mouth Rina. "Girl, you're so lucky. Your mom and dad take you everywhere. Not me. I get stuck at home all the time. My stepdad won't take me nowhere."

"*Cállate*, Rina," Tommy tells her. "Don't be a crybaby!"

Rina goes over to Tommy and slugs him. We all start to laugh. Then Tyrone mentions that Public Enemy is giving a concert next month in Santa Barbara. I'm relieved when everyone starts talking about music and forgets all about summer vacation.

When the warning bell rings for fifth period, I quickly grab my backpack and head toward campus before Tyrone has a chance to follow me. Juanita is right behind me.

When we get to our lockers, she says, "You're acting weird, Maya. Did you break up with Tyrone or what?"

"Don't be silly, Johnny," I answer, sharply. "We were never going together. We're just friends."

I can tell by the injured look on Juanita's face that I've hurt her feelings. But I know she's too good a friend to say anything mean to me. "Well," Juanita says, "I know Tyrone still likes you. I can tell by the way he was looking at you." This time I don't say anything. I grab my books and walk away, wishing Juanita would stay out of my business. Tyrone is the least of my problems. I don't really care what he thinks. For that matter, I don't care what any of them think. They're all so immature, joking around and acting like babies. Don't they know there are more important things to think about?

My fifth-period class turns out to be the worst class of the day. I can't seem to concentrate and I'm so glad when it's finally over and it's time for P.E. Mrs. Irving makes us run some laps around the track, and I feel the tension in my body start to disappear. Then we play tennis. I pair up with Rina and we spend the rest of the period playing doubles with some of the other girls.

After school, I walk over to the tennis courts for the first meeting of the Junior Varsity tennis team. I recognize the same girls from last year, with the exception of a few new freshmen. The coach is happy to see us. He gives us a big welcome and tells us that this year we're going to have a winning year and go all the way to the championship game. For the first time, I don't care about playing tennis or about being on the tennis team. I don't pay attention to what the coach is saying. I find myself thinking about Dad. He always used to come to my tennis matches. What will I do without him this year? How can I even play tennis, knowing he won't be there to watch me? I feel so empty now. I miss Dad more than ever. But maybe he'll call me tonight. Then I can tell him all about my first day as a junior.

✎   ✐   ✐

When I get home, Mom's Volvo is in the driveway, but I really don't care. The house seems empty now. Big and empty. As I step inside the living room, I can see Mom's feet propped up on the coffee table. She's sitting in her favorite chair watching Phil Donahue. Mom's feet are always aching. She says it's from standing and lecturing to college students all day.

When she hears me, she quickly turns her head to greet me. "Hi, *m'ija*. How was your first day as a junior? Did you go to your tennis meeting?"

"It was fine," I answer cooly, heading straight for my bedroom.

"Wait a minute, Maya," she calls after me. "I want you to sit and tell me all about your classes."

"Later, Mom. I'm really tired," I holler, slamming the bedroom door behind me.

I drop my backpack on the floor, turn the radio on, and let myself fall onto the bed. I wonder why I've been so rude to Mom? She was just trying to be nice. Maybe she's lonely, too, like me. I bury my head in my pillow, hoping Dad will call me tonight. Then I can tell him how much I miss him.

THREE
Maya

The first few weeks of school go by quickly, even though Dad still hasn't called me. Mom makes excuses for him, saying he's working long hours, but I don't believe her. I can tell she feels as miserable as I do in this big empty house. Sometimes at night, I can hear her crying softly in her room. But I really don't care. After all, Grandma was right. She's the one to blame for everything.

Most of my classes are boring, except for Spanish and Art. Mrs. Plumb actually seems happy to see all of us again, even though we torture her all year long with Spanish words she can't understand. And my Art class is fun. I love Art because I can lose myself in images and colors. Mrs. Patterson, the Art teacher, says I have a lot of talent in drawing. She's always showing my work off in class, and sometimes this embarrasses me. Ever since I can remember, I've loved art. My mom has a thing for Picasso and Frida Kahlo, so I grew up with their artwork all over the house.

At lunchtime, I keep on getting together with Juanita and the rest of the guys, but no matter how hard I try, I just can't seem to enjoy being a part of their group like before. I know Juanita can sense that I am feeling differently. She keeps asking me why I'm having little cows all the time. And every time she invites me to her house after school, I make up an excuse so that I don't have to go there. Juanita doesn't say anything, but I can see the hurt feeling in her eyes.

Even tennis seems boring and meaningless. I'm starting to hate going to practice every day. The coach is always getting on my case. The other day he jumped all over me just because I was fifteen minutes late. I can't stand him and all those stupid girls dressed in their little tennis skirts. I wonder what Dad would say if he knew that I hate tennis now.

One day after tennis practice while waiting at the corner for the city bus, I notice two weird-looking guys approach. I pretend I don't know them, but I recognize both. I don't know the name of the tall, long-haired guy with an earring, but I've seen him around the school campus. He belongs to the heavy-metal crowd at Roosevelt. They always wear black concert T-shirts and hang out in the parking lot after school. The short *cholo*-looking like guy next to him is in my Spanish class. His name is Charley Maestas. He drives Mrs. Plumb crazy because he never does his homework and he always answers her in *pachuco* talk. We all laugh when Mrs. Plumb takes out her dictionary and tries to look up the words Charley uses. She never finds a single one. Charley hangs out with the heavy-metal kids. I guess that explains his weird haircut.

Before I have time to react, Charley and his friend are standing next to me. *"Orale,* Maya. Have you got a light?" Charley asks.

Embarrassed, I look at Charley's round face and mumble, "Sorry, I don't smoke." I notice the small heart-shaped tattoo on Charley's right arm.

Charley turns to his tall friend and says, "I guess we'll have to sweat it out, Shane, till we get to the mall."

I can feel the tall guy stare at me, but I pretend that I'm looking down the road for the bus.

"You play tennis?" Shane suddenly asks me.

This time I'm compelled to turn and look directly into his face. As hard as I try, I can't help but feel intimidated by his piercing blue eyes and by his handsome face with the small cleft in the chin. I'm about to mumble an answer to Shane's question when Charley beats me to it.

"Hey, *ese,"* Charley says. "Maya's the only Chicana on the tennis team."

"That's cool," Shane answers, keeping his eyes fixed on me.

I'm beginning to feel more and more uncomfortable when the bus finally pulls up to the curb and rescues me. I grab my racket and climb onto the bus. The bus is packed with people at this time of day, and I'm forced to sit in the back next to a woman holding a baby. As the bus pulls away, I notice that Shane is staring up at my window. I feel like waving, but decide not to. All the way home, I find myself thinking about Shane and Charley, wondering what it would be like to hang out with them.

✎   ✏   ✐

A week later, I'm taking the long way through the parking lot to the tennis courts, late as usual, when a car pulls up next to me. When I look through the open window, I recognize Charley.

"*Orale*, Maya, wanna go cruising with us?" he asks me.

The pimple-faced guy in the driver's seat smiles at me. "I can't. I have practice," I answer, glancing sideways. Shane is sitting all alone in the back seat.

"Come on, Maya," Shane says firmly. "We'll show you a good time."

All of a sudden, my heart is beating faster. I can feel Shane staring up at me. Maybe it wouldn't hurt to miss practice just this once. After all, tennis is such a bummer. It would be exciting to do something different for a change. "Okay, I'll go," I hear myself answer in a voice I've never heard before.

Shane opens the door for me and scoots over to the other side of the back seat. "I have to be home by 5:30 or my mom will have a fit. Okay, Charley?" I ask, setting my bag between me and Shane.

"That's cool, *esa*," Charley answers back as the pimple-faced guy accelerates and drives out of the school parking lot.

I can feel my stomach start to cramp from nervousness. What am I thinking, getting into a strange car with guys I don't even know? And, especially heavy-metal guys, dopers, as everyone calls them.

"Wanna smoke, Maya?" Shane asks, waving a pack of Marlboros at me.

"No, thanks," I answer in a shaky voice. "I don't smoke." Out of the corner of my eye, I watch as Shane lights a cigarette.

"What kind of name is Maya, anyway?" he asks, inhaling deeply.

I still can't believe I'm doing this. I've always hated being around cigarette smoke, and now here I am suffocating in it. Shane is staring at me intensely, waiting for an answer to his question.

"Well, my mom is a sixties person, and I guess she was on some kind of Indian trip or something, so she talked my dad into naming me Maya."

I'm relieved when Shane doesn't ask me anything else. For the next few minutes, I pretend to look out the window until I notice that the pimple-faced guy is getting on the freeway. "Charley," I blurt out, "where are you guys headed?"

"Over to San Martin to the mall," Charley answers.

I'm starting to feel nauseated from all the cigarette smoke, so I roll the window down a little.

"Don't sweat it, *esa*," Charley tells me. "Spike here will have us back by 5:30. We're just gonna go hang out, meet some other guys."

The pimple-faced guy finally speaks. "Relax, babe," he tells me. Then he turns to Charley and says, "Hey, *cholo*, put Metallica on."

The music is blaring now. I feel my stomach start to cramp again and I wonder what I'm doing in this car, listening to heavy-metal music.

Shane's voice interrupts my thoughts. "Metallica's new release."

"Oh, yeah?" I mumble, pretending to sound interested.

A half-hour later, when we pull into San Martin, I'm beginning to feel a little less nervous.
Things could be worse. At least I'm not stuck at the
tennis courts with those stupid girls. It's sort of
exciting being in San Martin. It reminds me of
Santa Fe. There are brown faces everywhere, not
like Laguna where all you see are *gringos*.

At the mall, we hurry over to the Video Palace.
I know that I stick out like a sore thumb, dressed
in my polo shirt and tennis skirt, walking with
three long-haired guys.

The Video Palace is packed with teenagers,
mostly guys. Shane signals for us to follow him,
and we walk over to join two long-haired guys and
a strange looking girl who are standing at the back
of the room talking. The girl has shaved hair. She
eyes me suspiciously as they all greet each other.
When Shane introduces me, the weird girl says,
"How come she's dressed so prissy?"

I can feel my face turn red, but I don't say anything because Shane comes to my rescue. "Shut up,
Ruby. At least Maya's not a drop-out like you. She's
on the tennis team."

Ruby ignores Shane's sarcastic remarks and
quickly loops her arm around his waist. But Shane
pushes her arm away from him. Now I understand
why Ruby is so antagonistic toward me. She has a
definite thing for Shane.

The guys spend the next hour playing video
games while Ruby and I stand around and watch
them. I notice that Ruby stays as close as possible
to Shane. After a while, though, she comes over to
my side and asks me if I want to go out by the
snack bar to have a smoke. I tell her I don't smoke,

but she insists that I join her. By then, I'm so bored that I decide to go along with her.

We walk out of the Video Palace and find a bench to sit on by the snack bar. At first, I feel nervous about being with Ruby, but I soon find out that she's not so bad after all. On the outside, Ruby seems pretty hard-core, with all that make-up and weird haircut. But after talking with her, I realize she's not as tough as she acts. Ruby tells me she dropped out of school this year and lives with her mom on the Mexican side of San Martin. I actually start to wish I was more like her. She's so different, not boring like me. Even the clothes she wears are cool. Ruby even tells me her parents are divorced. By the time the guys join us, Ruby and I are talking away as if we'd known each other for years.

When we finally leave the mall, it's almost five o'clock. I start to feel worried again. What if Mom decides to swing by the tennis courts to give me a ride home and doesn't find me there? How will she react when the coach tells her I didn't go to practice? All the way back home, I imagine horrible things.

By the time we pull off the freeway into Laguna, I tell myself that I'll never do this again. When we get to my neighborhood, I tell the guys to drop me off two blocks from my house so Mom won't see me with them. Before I get out of the car, Shane pulls me to him and kisses me. I'm so excited that I don't even care about the awful cigarette taste on his lips. As the car pulls away, Shane waves goodbye to me.

As soon as I open the front door, Mom's voice greets me from the kitchen. "Is that you, Maya? Why are you so late? How was practice?"

I can tell from her cheerful tone that she doesn't suspect a thing. I feel a sudden relief. "Oh, fine," I lie, poking my head into the kitchen. She's standing in front of the stove, stirring something. Before she has time to ask me anything else, I tell her, "I smell like a pig. I need a shower badly," and I race downstairs to my bedroom.

FOUR
Maya

The next week, I start joining Shane and
Charley during lunchtime. At first, I make excuses
to Juanita and Rina about why I can't eat with
them, but after a while they see me with Shane, so
they stop bugging me. Usually, I meet Shane and
Charley in the parking lot, where we sit in some-
body's car and listen to heavy-metal music. Everyone stares at us, especially at me, since I don't
usually hang out with the heavy-metal crowd. But
I really don't care anymore.

It isn't long before I start ditching tennis practice so I can hang out with Shane and Charley. One
morning after a school assembly, I come face to face
with with Coach Harris and he asks me why I
haven't been to practice. I make up a story about
how my parents feel I need to spend more time on
schoolwork, but I can tell he's not convinced by the
explanation. I've always been straight with Coach
Harris and I feel bad about lying to him, but I
know I can't tell him the truth. He would call Mom
right away.

It's really exciting being with Shane and
Charley. When I'm with them, I forget about about
how much I miss my dad. Yet, I know he would kill

me if he knew what I was doing after school. Especially since most of the time we end up driving over to San Martin to hang out at the mall or at the city park.

Ruby and I are usually the only girls in the group. Now that Ruby knows me better, she doesn't act as tough, but she's still possessive about Shane. One time I asked Shane if Ruby used to be his girl-friend, but he laughed out loud and said, "Nah, she's just a chick, that's all." That made me feel pretty good, because I'm starting to like Shane more and more.

✎ ✐ ✐

One morning I am rushing back to my locker after my fourth period class when Juanita comes up behind me and grabs me by the arm.

"Wait up, Maya," she insists. "I want to talk to you."

I pretend to slow down, hoping that she'll disappear quickly.

"How come you don't want to hang out with us no more at lunchtime?" Juanita asks indignantly.

"I never said that," I answer cooly.

"And you never answer my calls. Why are you acting so stuck-up, Maya, ignoring us all the time?"

I stop walking and turn to look at Juanita. Her upper lip is quivering and her face is flushed. For a moment, I want to tell Juanita how much I'm hurting inside, how empty and lonely I've felt since my dad left. But something holds me back. I know I can't tell her the truth. Not now.

"Don't be stupid, Johnny," I tell her sarcastically. "I'm not ignoring anybody."

"Don't lie, Maya. I've seen you hanging out with those losers. I don't know what's the matter with you. They're nothing but trouble."

"If anyone is a loser, it's you, Johnny. You're the one who was kicked out of school for fighting, or did you forget that?"

A hurt look appears on Juanita's face and her eyes start to fill with tears. "Shut up, Maya," she mumbles before she turns and walks away in the opposite direction.

By the time I reach my locker, my eyes are watery. I can't understand why I was so mean to Juanita. She's always been so nice to me. Juanita was the first one to talk to me when I moved here from the Bay Area. She was the one who introduced me to Rina and Ankiza. And now, here I am treating her like a dog. What is the matter with me? Maybe I'm having a breakdown or something. I don't know. I only wish things could be like before. I slam my locker door behind me and hurry out of the building to meet Shane.

✎   ✐   ✐

That evening, I decide to try reaching Dad again at his new apartment in San Francisco. It rings and rings and I'm about to hang up when he finally answers.

"Hello," I hear him say in his familiar husky voice.

All of a sudden, I'm choking up inside. I start to imagine Dad's black curly hair and the two creases that run across his forehead.

"Hi, Dad, it's me, Maya," I finally whisper.

"Maya. Are you all right? It's pretty late to be calling."

"Yeah, I'm fine," I lie. There is a brief silence as I think about what I am going to say next. Finally, I blurt out, "Dad, I've been trying and trying to reach you. I really miss you. When can I come see you?"

"I've been meaning to call you, but I've been swamped at work."

"Dad, I really miss you. When can I come see you?"

"I miss you too, Maya, but you know, now is not a good time to come visit. I'm very busy at work, putting in these long hours. And well, I just can't take any days off right now."

There is a long pause. "Not even one weekend?" I ask.

"I'm sorry, honey, but I'm tied up for the next few weekends. We have this project we're working on. But you know, Thanksgiving vacation is coming up soon and maybe you can come then. I'll be more settled in the apartment by then."

I feel like crying again, but I force myself to hold back the tears. In a shaky voice, I hear myself say, "Sure, Dad. Well, I better hang up now. If Mom finds out I'm on the phone this late, she'll have a fit."

"Okay, honey. I'll call soon. Bye."

I wait until I hear the click at the other end of the line. Then I slam the receiver down so hard that the phone crashes to the floor. I bury my head in my pillow and cry myself to sleep.

FIVE
Maya

As the weeks go by, I start to feel less and less guilty about lying to Mom and to my friends, but one afternoon, as soon as I step inside the house, Mom is standing at the door waiting for me. "Where were you, Maya?" she yells at me.

I start to feel a tightening in my stomach. "At practice," I answer in a panicky voice.

"No, you weren't! You must think I'm stupid, right? Well, I went over to practice today and the coach told me that you quit going, that you gave him some story about having to study more."

My face is burning hot. I know that I've been busted.

"What a joke, studying more. Today I received your first quarter grades and you're failing three classes. Can you tell me what's going on, Maya?"

"Nothing," I answer defensively. "I just got bored with tennis. And the reason I have low grades in those classes is because the teachers are jerks."

My mother's face is flushed and her teeth are clenched. "I can't believe you're talking like this, Maya. You've always gotten along with your teach-

ers and you used to love tennis. I don't understand."

"People change, Mom. Just because you love
tennis doesn't mean I have to."

"Is it because of the divorce, Maya? Is that why
you're behaving like this?" my mom asks in disbelief.

"It has nothing to do with that." I shrug and
look down at my feet.

"And where, may I ask, have you been going
after school if you haven't been at tennis practice?"

I can feel another lie coming. I'm getting to be
an expert at it. "To the mall with my friends," I
answer, avoiding my mom's face.

"Well, all of that is going to stop from now on,
Maya. You're grounded, and I expect you to come
straight home every day after school. I also expect
you to do all the homework you obviously haven't
been doing. Is that understood?"

"You make me sick, Mom," I yell back at her.
Then I quickly step around her and run downstairs
to my room, locking the door behind me.

✎ ✐ ✐

For the next few days I start coming home
right after school. Mom even makes it a point to
call to make sure I'm home. Slowly, I start to feel
like a prisoner in my own home. I start to hate
Mom more than ever.

Then one day at lunchtime, I'm complaining to
Shane about being grounded when Charley gives
me an idea. "Why don't you sneak out of your room,
esa? Your mom would never know." The rest of the

day I keep thinking about Charley's idea of sneaking out, wondering whether I can get away with it. On Saturday I'm feeling so desperate to see Shane that I decide to try it. At exactly ten o'clock that evening, I tell Mom that I'm tired and that I'm going to bed. She says good night to me without suspecting a thing. I wait quietly in the dark until I hear her turn off the television and go to bed. I wait a while longer until I'm sure she is sound asleep. Then, I carefully take the screen off my bedroom window and climb out into the back yard. I tiptoe quietly around the house, open the front gate, and take off toward the next block to wait for Shane and the guys to pick me up. That night, I stay out until almost one o'clock while Mom sleeps through the entire thing.

During the weeks that follow, I continue sneaking out the window to be with Shane without Mom even suspecting. Sometimes I feel scared and I wonder if I'm going to get caught, but I quickly push these thoughts out of my mind. Then one evening I get into the worst trouble I have ever experienced. It all happens so fast, like in a movie, and the next thing I know my mom is racing into the Laguna police station looking for me. Her face is pale and she looks older than I've ever seen her look before.

"Maya, what is going on? Are you all right?" she asks, horrified.

Frightened, I start to cry and my mom puts her arms around me. The police officer who arrested me turns to Mom and says, "I'm sorry, Mrs. Gonzales. But your daughter was caught shoplifting this evening. But since she's a minor and this is her first offense, we can release her to you."

Mom gives a deep groan. She looks as if she's about to faint, so the officer helps her sit down. After a few minutes, she mumbles something to the officer and then signs a release form so I can leave with her.

In the car, I can tell Mom is still in shock because she doesn't say a word to me. I start to hate myself for doing this to her. I don't know why this had to happen. I don't know why I ever let Ruby talk me into stealing those clothes. I should have ignored her when she called me a chicken. I should have walked away from her.

When we get home, Mom orders me straight to bed. Later that night, I hear muffled cries coming from the family room. I wonder if she has called Dad. All that night I dream that Dad comes to visit me, but I am locked up behind bars.

SIX
Ms. Martínez

I had just stepped into the kitchen for a drink of water when the phone started to ring. It was almost 10:30. I wondered who could be calling this late at night. Thank goodness, Frank wasn't home yet. He hated those late night calls, especially when it was from one of my patients. Frank always scolded me for giving out my phone number so easily, but I teased him back about being an overprotective husband.

As I picked up the receiver, I couldn't help but think that maybe Frank was right about my late night calls. "Hello," I said, trying my best not to sound irritated.

"Hello, Sandy. It's Sonia. I'm sorry for calling so late."

There was a certain tension in Sonia's voice that I'd never heard before. Sonia was usually in control of things, but now something was definitely bothering her. "Oh, hello, Sonia. That's okay. You caught me right before I jumped into bed. I've been meaning to call you, but you know how it is, time just got away from me."

"Yes, I certainly know how that is," Sonia answered.

There was a moment of silence as I waited for
Sonia to continue speaking. Finally, I decided to
break the silence, hoping she would reveal her reason for calling so late at night.

"So how have you been, Sonia? How was your
trip to New Mexico?"

"Well, I don't know where to begin, Sandy. It's
about Maya. I need your help with her."

The next thing I heard were Sonia's muffled
sobs, and I knew that something terrible had happened.

"Sonia, what's wrong. Is Maya all right?" My
mind started to race back in time. It had been several months since my last counseling session with
Juanita. The last time we had talked, she and
Maya were both doing great.

"It's so hard for me to talk about it, Sandy,"
Sonia answered in an uneven voice. "But several
days ago Maya was caught shoplifting. And her
teachers have been calling me; she's failing most of
her classes. I'm on the verge of a nervous breakdown, Sandy. I just don't know how to handle her
anymore."

Sonia was crying softly in the background
again. I thought back to my conversations with
Juanita and how many times she had repeated
enviously, "Maya is so perfect. She has the perfect
family, the perfect house." What could possibly
have happened to shatter Juanita's illusion?

"Sonia, you need to get hold of yourself," I insisted in a mother-like tone. "Is Maya home right
now?"

"Yes. She's here," Sonia answered in a muffled
voice. "I've grounded her again, but I don't think
it's doing much good. I just can't seem to get

through to her anymore. That's why I'm calling you."

This was the first time I had ever heard Sonia sound so helpless. She was usually very sure of herself.

"I'm really sorry to hear all of this, Sonia," I said calmly. "Why don't we meet for lunch tomorrow and talk. We can go over to the little Chinese restaurant. We haven't done that in a long time."

"Okay," Sonia answered, sounding more hopeful. "Tomorrow is a good day for me. I only have two morning classes."

"Good. Then I'll see you there at noon, okay?"

"Okay. And Sandy, thanks."

The next morning, as I finished up with my last patient, I kept thinking about my luncheon appointment with Sonia. Of all my professional friends, Sonia was the one I admired the most—Stanford Ph.D., yearly trips to Europe, gorgeous house, gorgeous husband. I remembered how impressed I had been when I first met her two years ago at a reception for the famous Chicano artist José Montoya. Sonia had given a brilliant introduction on Chicano Art. Later, she had walked over and introduced herself to me. From that day on, we had developed a close friendship, especially since we were the only Chicana professionals in Laguna.

When I walked into the Chinese restaurant, Sonia was already waiting for me at a table in the back corner. I waved and hurried over to meet her. "Hope I'm not horribly late," I said, sitting down across from her. Sonia didn't look as pretty today as she usually did. Her dark-brown wavy hair hung limp around her shoulders and there were dark circles around her eyes that made her look older.

Before Sonia had time to say anything, the waitress appeared with a pot of tea.

"Shall we have some tea first and talk for a while before we order?" I asked her.

"Sure," Sonia answered quietly.

As soon as the waitress disappeared I asked Sonia point-blank, "Okay, Sonia, tell me what's going on."

Sonia's eyes filled with tears as she began to speak. "It's Maya. She's totally out of control. I can't seem to handle her anymore."

"In what way is she out of control?" I asked, trying my best to sound sympathetic. Lately, it seemed like every parent I talked with seemed to think their kids were out of control.

"Well, for one thing, she's failing most of her classes. Then I found out she quit the tennis team and she's been hanging out with these bums. And to top it off, she was caught stealing."

"That certainly doesn't sound like Maya," I said, handing Sonia a Kleenex from my purse. "Did she tell you why she was stealing?"

"Well," Sonia answered, groping for the right words, "she said that one of her friends dared her, so she had to do it. She's hanging out with this rough group of kids. I guess the girl who dared her is from San Martin."

I waited for a few moments while Sonia blew her nose, knowing that I needed to be careful how I phrased the next question. "Sonia, when teenagers suddenly start to behave in extreme ways, there's usually a reason behind it. Now, I know this is a difficult question, but is there anything going on at school or at home that might have caused Maya's sudden behavior change?"

Sonia let out a deep breath. I could feel the tension mounting inside of her as I waited patiently for her to answer. "Armando moved out this summer. We're getting a divorce."

Suddenly, everything seemed to fall into place. "I'm very sorry, Sonia," I replied, reaching over and patting her on the hand. "Why didn't you let me know sooner?"

"Oh, I guess I was embarrassed. I don't know. We both agreed it was for the best. It was a friendly separation."

A friendly separation? Who was Sonia trying to kid? There was no such thing. I remembered my own divorce from Raúl and how it had hurt my entire family.

"Sonia, divorce is one of the most difficult things for families to cope with, especially teenagers. And the tendency is to think that because teenagers are older, they adapt much easier to a divorce. But it doesn't happen like that."

"I guess I fooled myself into thinking that Maya was handling it okay, but now it's obvious she's turned into a complete stranger."

"Have you been able to talk to her about the divorce, about her feelings?" I asked.

"I've been trying, but she won't listen to me. She says it's all my fault. You know how she idolizes her dad."

"Has Armando tried talking with her?"

"Are you kidding?" Sonia asked sarcastically. "He never calls her. She hasn't seen him in months."

"Where is he living?"

"He's back in the Bay Area. And he keeps saying he's going to have Maya up for a visit, but every time she asks him about it, he says it's a bad weekend or that he's too busy."

The waitress appeared, interrupting our conversation. "Are you ready to order?" she asked impatiently.

"What shall we order, Sonia?" I said, scanning the menu.

"It doesn't matter. The usual, I guess. I'm not very hungry."

"You, not hungry. ¿Estás loca?" I teased. Sonia's face began to relax, revealing a half-smile. Good. I had made her smile. I wasn't used to seeing Sonia look depressed. She was always the cheerful one, telling funny stories about her college students.

After we had finished ordering, Sonia was the first to speak. "What really worries me, Sandy, is the fact that she was stealing. She has to appear in court next month. I'm really embarrassed by the whole thing. Most of all, I'm scared. Scared for Maya. Why in the world would she steal if she already has everything?"

Like most of my patients, Sonia obviously wasn't getting it. She was too blinded by her own emotional problems. "There are reasons for everything, Sonia. It's clear to me just from the little you've told me that Maya is hurting on the inside and this is her way of acting that out."

Sonia's eyes were quickly filling with tears. "You think so, Sandy? I guess that's why I wanted to talk with you. What should I do?"

"I think you both need counseling."

"I already suggested that to Maya and she told me where to go," Sonia explained. "But I know how much she likes you, so I was wondering if you would talk with her."

I hesitated before answering. As a general rule, I never liked to counsel my friends and their families. It's easier to keep my personal feelings separate from my professional life.

"Please, Sandy. I know she'll listen to you. She thinks the world of you."

I had never been able to resist Sonia's pleas for help. I guess that's why we were *compañeras*, marching together in support of the United Farm Workers' union, serving on panels, you name it. Only this time, Sonia was the one who needed help.

"All right, Sonia," I said. "But Maya has to agree to come and see me. You can't force her. She has to want to come and talk with me on her own."

A look of relief appeared on Sonia's tired face. "Thanks, Sandy. I know I can convince Maya to see you. She admires you so much."

"Good. But I recommend that you get some help for yourself as soon as possible. I can recommend a good therapist. Divorce is not an easy thing to deal with on your own." Who should know better than me? The memories of my own divorce still haunted me even after all these years.

"I will, Sandy. I promise I'll look into it right away," Sonia said, interrupting my thoughts.

"Good. Then it's all settled. Now we can pig out. Oh, I forgot. You're not hungry, right?"

"*Cállate*," Sonia scolded me as the waitress set the steaming plates on our table.

SEVEN
Ms. Martínez

That evening, I had trouble sleeping. The memories of my divorce from Raúl came back to haunt me. Raúl, the tall, handsome green-eyed Chicano who had been my first love. We had started dating during my senior year in high school. One night after a football game, I was walking home with my girlfriends when Raúl pulled up in his blue '64 Falcon and asked me if I wanted to go cruise around town with him. I was as taken by surprise as my girlfriends, who all had crushes on him.

I went out with Raúl that night, and from then on we were inseparable. All through high school, I had had my share of crushes on different guys, but I had never fallen hopelessly in love with anyone like I did with Raúl. We spent every possible minute of our senior year together. Every morning, Raúl would pick me up a few blocks from my house and we would ride to school together. I was the envy of all my girlfriends. At lunchtime, we would meet in the parking lot and sit in Raúl's car listening to the radio and making out. Then after school, we would meet again and cruise around town for a while before Raúl drove me home. I remember how every evening I would wait impatiently for the phone to ring so that I could talk with him again.

My parents never knew I was dating Raúl. I wanted so badly to tell them about him, but I knew it was wishful thinking since they had made it clear that I couldn't date until I turned eighteen. My only resort was to sneak around and lie to my parents so that I could be with him. Instead of going to a game or to a friend's house, as I had told them, I'd wait for Raúl to pick me up, and we would drive out to the country roads and park.

At first, the only thing Raúl and I did when we were together was make out. But then Raúl became more insistent. One night, we let our passion overcome us. I remember feeling guilty and embarrassed afterward because I knew it was wrong, but Raúl's promises to marry me made it seem all right. And I loved Raúl so much that I didn't want to lose him.

Finally, the worst thing possible happened. My mother caught me sneaking out the window to meet Raúl. When I told her that Raúl and I were in love and planning to get married, she slapped me and threatened to hit me with the belt if I ever went out with him again. She forbade me to see Raúl, telling me that if my father found out he would kill me. I was furious. I couldn't believe this was happening to me. Here I was seventeen years old and not even allowed to go out on dates.

I decided that night that I wouldn't let anything keep me apart from Raúl. I formed a plan with Raúl's help and then I waited patiently to carry it out. When graduation day arrived, I packed some clothes in a small bag and smuggled them out of the house. After my graduation party, I waited until my parents were asleep and then I quietly fled from the house with Raúl, who was waiting for me at the corner.

We stayed at Raúl's brother's house that night, and after a few days my parents came looking for me. But I refused to go back home, insisting that Raúl and I belonged together. A few weeks later, my parents finally relented. Raúl and I were married the following month in a small church ceremony.

At first, it was fun playing house while Raúl worked construction and I stayed home cooking and cleaning the small apartment. On weekends, Raúl and I had wild parties with our friends and stayed up as late as we wanted. We were ecstatic with our new independence. But after the first year had passed, I began to notice that Raúl and I didn't really know each other. Unlike Raúl, who was satisfied with getting a pay check and partying every weekend, I started to feel restless and confined in the small apartment. I needed more things to occupy my time, but when I told Raúl, he would ignore me. We started disagreeing about everything, and when I enrolled in an evening class at a nearby university, Raúl was furious. He started to spend more time drinking with his buddies after work, leaving me alone at home.

Our relationship continued like this for several more years until I couldn't take it anymore. Raúl's drinking had worsened and we had become complete strangers to one another. When I finally made up my mind to leave him, my parents became angry, even though they had disapproved of our marriage from the start. My mother yelled at me,

"Sandra, are you out of your mind? God will curse you if you get a divorce." My mother never quite forgave me for leaving Raúl. She could never accept the fact that her only daughter was not only divorced, but pursuing a career. That was totally unacceptable. Catholics are never supposed to get divorced. It was "until death do us part." No wonder Sonia was a mess. Divorce was a devastating experience for the entire family.

EIGHT
Ms. Martínez

On Wednesday afternoon I was getting ready to leave my office when I heard a light knock on the door. I glanced at my appointment book, thinking I had overlooked someone. I had purposely not scheduled anyone after four o'clock that day so that I could get home early for a change. God, I hoped it wasn't a walk-in.

I debated whether I should open the door or wait for the knocking to stop, but, as usual, my strong sense of responsibility won out. When I opened the door, I found Juanita standing there waiting.

"Juanita, what a nice surprise," I explained in disbelief. "Come in. I haven't seen you in months. How are you?"

"Hi, Ms. Martínez," Juanita replied, stepping inside my office. "Sorry I didn't call first. I was walking by and I felt like seeing you."

"How nice. Have a seat. I've missed talking with you."

"Yeah, me too," Juanita said, sitting down at the far end of the couch. "I wanted to come see you this summer, but I went to work with my dad in the fields, so I didn't have time."

"How are your mom and dad doing?"

"Oh, they're real good. They always say to tell you hi."

"And how's school coming along this year? Every now and then I talk to Sam Turner and he always asks for you."

My thoughts drifted back to the previous year. It had been a long battle, but Sam and I had succeeded in getting Juanita reinstated in school. I would be forever grateful to Sam. If he hadn't donated his services as an attorney, we would have never convinced the school board to let Juanita return to school.

"It's real good, Ms. Martínez," Juanita answered. "I'm just so glad to be back. I never want to get kicked out again."

"Good girl. And don't forget, Sam and I want an invitation to your graduation next year."

"I won't forget, Ms. Martínez," Juanita promised.

"Are you still seeing Rudy?" I asked.

Juanita blushed. "Yeah, we're still going out."

"Well, just remember to be careful, okay? Remember everything we talked about."

"I will. You don't have to worry about me no more, Ms. Martínez."

"Good."

The room filled with silence as I waited for Juanita to speak. All of a sudden, she sat straight up and started pulling nervously on the hem of her short skirt. I sensed that she had come here to talk about something that was bothering her.

"How is everything else going?" I asked Juanita gently.

Juanita looked up at me with her dark oval-shaped eyes. She hesitated for a moment and then blurted out, "Well, I kinda wanted to see you 'cause I needed some advice about something."

Good. We were finally getting somewhere. "Sure, Juanita. Can you tell me what it's all about?"

"Well, it's about Maya. She used to be my best friend, but now she's acting all hot. She doesn't want to talk to me no more. And she never comes to my house. She started hanging out with these creeps, some heavy-metal guys. I'm really worried about her."

I wished I could tell Juanita about my recent conversation with Sonia, but I knew that I couldn't. I had to act as if I knew nothing about Maya's recent behavior change.

"Have you tried talking with Maya, asking her if something is bothering her?"

"Yeah, we've all tried. Rina, Tommy, even Tyrone. Tyrone used to be her boyfriend. But she won't talk to him no more. She keeps ignoring all of us. She won't even eat lunch with us no more."

Juanita's eyes were filling with tears and I could tell that Maya's behavior was hurting her deeply.

I reached over and patted her hand. "It sounds to me like something is bothering Maya, for her to act so differently. I'm sure she doesn't mean to hurt you, Juanita. Sometimes things happen to people and they have a hard time coping with their new feelings. Many times they end up hurting the people closest to them without even knowing it."

"Well, what do you think I should do, Ms. Martínez?" Juanita asked hopefully. "I really miss Maya."

"The best thing you can do is continue to be Maya's friend even if it looks as if she doesn't care. When people are hurting inside, they need all the love and support they can get, and it sounds to me like Maya is hurting."

"I was kinda wondering if maybe you could talk to her, Ms. Martínez. You helped me so much last year with the fight and everything."

"Juanita, Maya has to want to come and see me. We can't force her. She needs to want to be helped."

"Yeah, I guess so," Juanita said. "I'll keep trying to talk with her. Maybe I can get through to her."

"Maya is very fortunate to have a good friend like you, Juanita," I said, getting up from my desk. "And now, I better get home before Frank calls the state police. Can I give you a ride home?"

"Sure, Ms. Martínez," Juanita said, standing up. "And thanks for everything."

✎ ✐ ✏

Later that evening, I dialed Sonia's number.

"Hello," Sonia answered, sounding tired and distant.

"Sonia, it's Sandy. I hadn't heard from you so I thought I'd check back to see how things were going with Maya."

"Thanks, Sandy. I was getting ready to call you. I've tried and tried to convince Maya to go and talk with you, but she won't listen to me. She insists that she doesn't need a 'shrink,' as she put it. I just don't know what to do anymore."

"I was afraid that would happen, Sonia. Maybe she needs some more time to sort things out. Maya is a smart girl. I'm sure she'll come around eventually. But what about yourself? Did you make that appointment?"

"Yes, I did. And I'm so glad that I did because it really helps talking to someone about the divorce."

"I knew it would help."

"But it's not me I'm worried about," Sonia quickly added. "It's Maya. She's shutting me out completely and I feel like we've become strangers."

"Be patient with her, Sonia. She's going through a lot of emotional changes right now."

"I know. It's just that we've always been so close."

"Well, as I said, Maya has a lot to sort out right now. Don't give up on her. Give her some time. But, meanwhile, take care of yourself. And remember, if and when Maya is ready to talk, I'll be here waiting."

"Thanks, Sandy. I didn't mean to dump all of this on you."

"Are you kidding?" I teased. "Isn't that what *comadres* are for?"

I heard Sonia laugh in the background and I had a sudden feeling of relief. "Well, time to go. I promised Frank I wouldn't be on the phone all night."

"Thanks for everything, Sandy," Sonia repeated as I hung up the receiver.

NINE
Maya

When I meet Shane at lunchtime, he tells me that tonight is teen night at the Rock. Then he asks me if I can sneak out just one more time. I feel so desperate to go out with Shane. Ever since my mom grounded me, I haven't dared sneak out the window. I don't know whether I should do it or not, but I really want to be with Shane. He's the only one who understands me.

That evening, I wait until I'm sure Mom is sound asleep before I carefully take the screen off my bedroom window and climb out into the back yard. I slowly grope along in the dark until I reach the gate that opens to the street. Then I hurry over to wait on the street corner where Shane and Charley are supposed to pick me up.

Scary thoughts race through my mind as I stand waiting next to the street light. What if Shane and Charley forget to pick me up? What if Mom wakes up and comes looking for me? I am starting to feel very panicky when all of a sudden a car comes screeching around the corner. I breathe a sigh of relief when I recognize Charley driving his dad's car. They pull up next to me

"Hey, babe," Shane greets me as I climb into the front seat between him and Charley. "We've been cruising around here for an hour watching for you. What took you?"

Before I can say anything, Shane tells Charley, "Let's hit it over to the Rock, Charley. See what's going down there."

I start to feel excited about going to the Rock. I haven't been there in such a long time. I wonder how it will feel dancing with Shane.

When we reach downtown, it takes us a while to find a parking spot. Since Laguna is the only university city in this area, the downtown is filled with fancy restaurants and dance clubs, like the Rock, that cater to the tourists and the university students. Mom hates coming downtown because it's impossible to find a parking space and she always runs into her students.

As soon as we get inside the Rock, I see a couple of the girls from the tennis team, but I pretend that I don't notice them. I hate those rich, stuck-up socies with a passion. That's what everyone calls them at school because they act so stuck-up.

"Let's go boogie," Shane says, pulling me onto the dance floor.

I'm surprised to find that Shane is a good dancer. I guess I always thought heavy-metal guys didn't dance, especially to hip-hop music. We dance for almost a half-hour and then head back toward the entrance where Charley is standing talking to some weird-looking guys I've never seen before. Shane joins their conversation, and I try to act as if I'm interested in what they're saying, even though I couldn't care less. All of a sudden, I feel someone tap me on the shoulder. I turn around and find myself face to face with Tyrone.

"Hi, Maya. Wanna dance?" he asks me.

My face is flushed. "No, thanks," I answer indignantly, turning away from him and moving closer to Shane, who hasn't even noticed that another guy has asked me to dance. Out of the corner of my eye, I watch as Tyrone turns and walks away from me to join Tommy, Rina and Juanita, who are standing on the other side of the dance floor waiting for him. From the look on Tyrone's face, I know that I've hurt him. Maybe I should have danced with him just once.

After a while, Shane pulls me back onto the dance floor. We keep dancing until the music finally stops and the lights go on signaling that it's closing time. Then we go back and join Charley and his weird friends.

We are walking out of the building when I hear someone call my name. It's Juanita. I'm not sure whether I should talk to her or not, but I find myself slowing down while Shane and Charley walk ahead of me.

"Hi, Maya. Can we talk?" Juanita asks in a subdued tone.

"About what?" I ask, trying to sound as rude as possible.

"I just wanted to talk, that's all."

Shane is waving at me and calling me to hurry. "Yeah, well, sorry, I'm in a hurry," I tell her, rushing away to catch up with Shane and Charley.

After cruising around Laguna for a while, we
get bored and drive out to the nearest beach where
we meet a couple of Charley's friends from the
dance. We crank up our car radios and lay some
blankets on the sand so we can all sit together.
Charley's weird friends have some beer with them.
I've never tasted beer before, but I make myself
drink one so they won't think I'm a baby. It tastes
bitter and it makes me feel so dizzy that I stay as
close as possible to Shane.

A while later, Shane asks me to go for a walk
with him on the beach. I can tell that he's had too
much to drink because he's talking weird. After we
walk up the beach a ways, we find a place to sit
and watch the waves. Shane puts his arms around
me, pressing his body up against mine, and I start
to feel warm all over. First he kisses me lightly,
then more deeply. I've never made out with a guy
like this before. When Shane starts to kiss me on
the neck, I panic. I abruptly push his hands away,
telling him that I feel sick to my stomach and need
to use the bathroom. Shane seems upset, but he
gives in and we walk back toward the cars.

When we finally get back to Laguna, it's
almost two in the morning. Shane insists on getting out of the car and walking me to my house.
When we get to the gate, Shane follows me into the
back yard. I'm afraid to argue with him because I
know he's had too much to drink. As soon as we get
to my bedroom window, I tell him goodbye and
sneak back inside my room. The next thing I know,
he crawls in through the window after me. I insist
that he leave, but he won't listen to me. Although it
is pitch dark, he manages to reach over and pull
me onto the bed with him. I am struggling to get

free from his grasp when suddenly the door bursts open and the room is filled with light.

"What is going on here?" Mom yells.

Shane immediately stands up, looking deathly pale.

"What the hell are you doing in my daughter's bedroom?" Mom asks Shane between clenched teeth.

"Wait, Mom, I can explain," I mumble, knowing that I'm in deep trouble.

"Shut up, Maya. And you, you better get out of this room before I call the police."

"Yeah, sure," Shane answers in a shaky voice.

"Where do you live?" Mom asks, glaring at Shane.

"On the other side of town."

"Well, get out of here before I have you arrested."

I start to speak, but before I have time to say anything, Mom reaches over and slaps me on the face as hard as she can. "You stay right here, Maya. I'll show him out."

I am so stunned by the sudden blow that I don't say anything. I watch in silence as Shane follows Mom down the hallway. My cheek is burning. This is the first time that my mom has ever hit me.

After a few minutes, Mom comes back into my room. I notice her eyes are red and puffy and she looks very old. But I don't care. I hate her. I can't stand looking at her. That's probably why Dad left. Maybe he couldn't stand looking at her either.

"Maya, how could you do this to me?" Mom asks me in an anguished voice.

"I didn't do anything," I say defensively, trying to convince myself that she is the bad person, not me.

"Aren't you ashamed, sneaking a boy into your room? I want you to know that you're grounded for life. And I'm calling your dad in the morning."

"I hate you. I can't stand you," I scream back at her. "It's all your fault Dad left. I hate you so much." I can feel the tears rolling down my cheeks.

Mom's eyes are filled with tears, but I can tell that she's trying to remain calm. "It's late and we're both too upset to talk now, Maya. Go to bed. We'll talk about this in the morning. And leave your bedroom door open!"

After she leaves, I cry myself to sleep, wishing things could be like before, wishing Dad were here.

✎   ✐   ✐

As soon as I wake up the next morning, I know what I have to do. I can hear the television in the family room, so I know Mom is already awake. I dress quickly, grab my purse, and head for the living room, hoping that my mom won't hear me. I'm almost at the front door when she suddenly appears before me. She grabs me by the arm and says, "Maya, where do you think you're going? You have a lot of explaining to do after what happened last night."

I push her away from me. "I can't stand being here anymore. And I can't stand being around you. I'm leaving," I yell at her, racing out the front door before she has time to stop me.

"*M'ija*, wait. Come back here," I hear her call out to me as I take off down the street.

TEN
Maya

By the time I reach the Town and Country Mall, my feet are starting to ache. I stop for a moment and watch the traffic going in and out of the mall. I don't know whether I should go into the mall or keep on walking. I don't know what I should do or where I should go. I only know I can't go back home. I can feel my eyes start to fill with tears, but I won't let myself cry now, not here in front of all these strangers staring at me from their car windows. I wonder if they know that I'm running away from home? If they know how much I hate my life?

I continue walking on Laguna road past the mall for almost an hour until I find myself in the downtown area. I have never walked this far before. My mom always warns me about how dangerous it is to walk alone like this, that someone might try to kidnap me. I start to wonder what Mom is doing right now. What if she called the police? What if they come and take me away to jail? Tears spring to my eyes again. Why did I do such a stupid thing? Now where will I go? What will I do? I wish Dad were here. I feel so alone. I've never run away from home before.

When I come to the 7-Eleven on the corner of Palm Street, I stop and stare at the phone booth in front of the entrance. Maybe I should call Mom. Maybe she'll forgive me. I open the door to the phone booth and reach for the receiver, but something holds me back. I know that I can't call her, not now, maybe never. Suddenly, Juanita's face flashes before me. I remember how she wanted to talk to me last night, but I wouldn't listen to her. Juanita's always stuck by me, even lately when I've been so hateful with her. Maybe I should call her. Maybe I can talk to Juanita, tell her about the fight with my mom.

All of a sudden, I find myself dialing Juanita's number. It rings and rings and I am about to hang up when a tiny little voice finally answers, "Who is it?"

Before I have time to say anything, I hear Juanita shout in the background, "Lupita, give me the phone! " Then Juanita is on the line.

I take a deep breath and say, "Johnny, it's me, Maya."

"Oh, hi," Juanita answers. "How come you sound so far away?"

"That's because I'm at a phone booth," I whisper.

"Maya, what's wrong? Your mom called earlier asking if I had heard from you. She called Rina and Ankiza, too."

I try to speak but my voice falters, and before I know it, I'm crying.

"Maya, what's the matter?" Juanita repeats.

In between the sobs, I explain to Juanita that I've run away from home. Juanita gasps, *"Híjole,"* and then asks me where I am calling from. As soon as I tell her that I'm downtown at the 7-Eleven, not too far from her family's apartment, she insists on coming to meet me. After we hang up, I feel better. I feel like I'm not alone anymore.

Fifteen minutes later I spot Johnny walking down the street toward me. I hurry to meet her and she gives me a hug, saying, "Listen, Maya. You're coming to my house. And don't worry, *Amá* and *Apá* aren't there. They're working today. Carlos went with them, too. Just me, Celia, and the three little ones are there."

"Thanks, Johnny," I tell her, tears streaming down my face. "But I wouldn't blame you if you didn't talk to me after the way I've been acting."

"Don't be silly. Friends stick together," Juanita says, hooking her arm around mine, just like old times.

✎   ✐   ✐

When we get to Juanita's apartment, Celia and the three little ones—Rosario, Lupita, and Markey—are playing catch in the front yard. Juanita lives in the low-income apartments in the part of Laguna that everyone calls the *barrio*. This is where most of Laguna's Chicanos, African-Americans, and Puerto Ricans live.

As soon as Markey spots us, he comes running up to me and I bend down to pick him up, forgetting all about my problems for a few minutes. Markey is the baby in Juanita's family and he's so lovable.

"Hi, Markey. How about a kiss?" I ask, and Markey gives me a sticky kiss on the lips. Then he starts squirming to get down, so I let go of him.

Juanita turns to Celia and tells her, "Maya and I will be upstairs. Don't bother us." Celia glares at Juanita. She hates it when Juanita bosses her around.

"Juanita, you're so lucky to have brothers and sisters," I tell her, feeling all alone again.

"Are you kidding?" Juanita says as we step inside the living room. "They're a real pain. They never leave you alone. Come on, let's go usptairs."

I follow Juanita upstairs to the small bedroom she shares with Celia. As soon as we are sitting down on her bed, Juanita turns to me and says, "Come on, Maya, tell me what happened."

I'm choking up inside as I start to speak. "My mom and I had a big fight. Last night she busted me sneaking back into my bedroom through the window. Shane was with me. But I swear we weren't doing anything. Shane had a couple of beers and he was kind of high, so he followed me into my room, that's all. But my mom had a big fit. So this morning I just couldn't stand it anymore, so I ran away."

A worried look appears on Juanita's face. "Maya, you can't run away from your problems. I know, 'cause I learned that the hard way last year, remember? And I know your mom loves you a lot. She's probably all worried right now."

"I can't stand her. It's all her fault," I whisper, wiping the tears away with the back of my hand.

"What's all her fault?"

"My dad moved out during the summer. They're getting a divorce. And my mom's the one to blame." There, I had finally said the word. Divorce.

I can tell by the startled look on Juanita's face that she's surprised by my sudden revelation. "Oh,

Maya. I'm really sorry. I didn't know," she whispers gently.

"Yeah, well, I didn't want anyone at school to know about it. But I really miss my dad."

Now the tears are streaming down my face. Juanita hands me some Kleenex and says, "Maya, I know your mom loves you a lot. But you just can't run away from home. I really need you here. You're my best friend."

This time I manage a faint smile. Juanita always knows how to make me feel good inside. Maybe she's right about Mom. Anyway, where can I run away to? To Dad's in San Francisco? I've always hated big cities and it's scary changing schools again, making new friends. "I don't know what I'll do, Johnny," I blurt out. "It's all pretty scary." I feel the tears rolling down my cheeks again.

"Don't cry, Maya," Johnny says, handing me another Kleenex. "We'll figure something out. Are you hungry? How about a *taco* ? I know you love *Amá's* tortillas and beans.

I had forgotten all about my empty stomach. "Yeah, I'm starved. I love your mom's beans," I answer.

"Okay. I'll be right back," Juanita says, leaving me alone in the room.

I lie back on the pillows, suddenly realizing how tired I am after all the walking I've done. I start to think about Mom. Juanita's right. She's probably really worried by now. And mad, too. I guess I really hurt her saying those awful things. I wonder if she's already called Dad?

Before I have time to worry some more, Juanita comes back into the room. "Here," she says, handing me a taco as I sit back up on the bed.

"Maya," Juanita says as she watches me eat. "I have an idea. What if we call Ms. Martínez and ask her for help. Remember how much she helped me last year?"

"I don't know," I answer, hesitating. "My mom kept trying to talk me into seeing her, but I said no. You know what I think of shrinks."

"*Ay*, Maya! Ms. Martínez is different. She's really nice, and if anyone can help, it's her. I know you're scared to go back home. I think talking with Ms. Martínez would help."

I remember the night Mom suggested I go see Ms. Martínez. I wouldn't hear of it. I had yelled at her, insisting all shrinks were stupid and that it was a stupid idea. But I was only trying to make Mom mad. Juanita is right. Ms. Martínez is pretty cool. If it weren't for her, Juanita wouldn't be back in school.

"Come on, Maya," Juanita begs. "Let me call Ms. Martínez. She told me to call her at home anytime I need something."

I don't know what I should do. I am so confused. But maybe Juanita is right. Maybe Ms. Martínez can help. "Okay. Go ahead and call her," I mumble.

"*Orale*! I'll call her right now," Juanita yells, disappearing out of the room before I have time to change my mind.

ELEVEN
Ms. Martínez

I heard the telephone ring and was debating with myself whether I should get up from my comfortable chair to answer it when I heard Frank pick up the receiver. "Martínez-Burton residence. Oh, hello, Juanita. Sure. I'll get her. Hon, it's for you," Frank called out to me.

I hurried into the kitchen, surprised that Juanita was calling me at home. As I reached for the phone, Frank whistled at me.

"Cut it out," I said, frowning at him as he disappeared into the garage. Sometimes Frank picked the worst moments to tease me.

"Hello," I said into the receiver.

"Hi, Ms. Martínez. It's me, Juanita."

"What a nice surprise. How are you?"

"I'm doing good, Ms. Martínez, but I called you 'cause I really need your help."

"Sure, Juanita. What's the matter?"

"Well, it's not me. It's Maya. She ran away from home this morning and she's here at my house."

"I'm really sorry to hear all of this," I said sympathetically. I immediately thought about Sonia and how terrible she must have been feeling.

"Yeah, me too," Juanita answered. "I was wondering if you weren't real busy, if you could come over and talk to Maya. She really needs to talk to you."

"Are you sure Maya wants to talk to me?" I asked in a firm voice, remembering my recent conversation with Sonia about how Maya had refused to get counseling.

"Yeah, I asked her and she said it was okay to call you. Just me, Celia, and the three little ones are home. Can you come over?"

It was obvious that Juanita was very concerned about Maya's well-being. I couldn't help but think how fortunate Maya was to have a friend like Juanita. "All right. Tell Maya I'll be there in fifteen minutes."

"Thanks, Ms. Martínez. I'll go tell, Maya."

I hung up the receiver and went out to the garage to let Frank know that I would be gone for about an hour.

✎ ✉ ✐

When I arrived at Juanita's apartment, I could hear the television blaring through the open door. Before I had time to knock, the screen door opened and Celia greeted me, "Hi, Ms. Martínez. Come in." For a moment I thought it was Juanita. She had the same oval-shaped eyes and long black hair.

"Hi, Celia," I said, stepping inside the small living room. Then I said hello to Markey, Lupita, and Rosario who were sitting together on the faded carpet watching cartoons. Every time I visited Juanita, I was amazed at how a family with six children could live in such a small apartment. Yet, with the high cost of housing, I knew this was a way of life for many of California's migrant workers.

I was about to ask Celia how her freshman year was coming along when Juanita walked into the room. "Hi, Ms. Martínez," she said cheerfully. Maya was standing behind her, trying her best not to look directly at me.

"Hello, Juanita. Hello, Maya," I said, gently.

"Hi, Ms. Martínez," Maya muttered, looking up at me. Her eyes were swollen and her long brown hair was hanging limp.

"Okay, *mocosos,*" Juanita said, turning off the television. "Everyone upstairs. Celia and I are going to play hide and seek with you." Juanita grabbed Markey by the hand and they all followed her upstairs.

I found a comfortable spot on the couch and watched quietly as Maya plopped herself down on the floor with her long skinny legs. It was amazing how much Maya resembled Sonia, with the same high Indian cheekbones and the exotic-looking dark skin. I waited patiently for Maya to speak. Finally, I decided to break the silence. "Maya, Juanita told me what happened. I'm very sorry about all of this. I know you must be feeling pretty miserable."

Maya's soft brown eyes started to fill with tears. "Yeah, I feel so bad," she whispered in a voice barely audible. "But I guess I was kind of mean to my mom."

"Your mom must be very worried about you, Maya, not knowing where you might have gone."

Maya bowed her head. "Yeah, I guess so, but she really makes me mad. Sometimes I feel like punching her."

I could feel the anger that had been building up inside Maya and I knew she was about to explode. "Can you tell me what it is that's making you feel this way, Maya?" I asked, carefully.

Maya was looking up at me now, tears streaming down her face. "She kicked my dad out. It's all her fault they're getting a divorce."

I reached over and handed Maya a Kleenex from my purse. "You know, Maya, divorce is really a difficult thing to cope with, especially for teenagers. I know it really hurts and I can tell that it's tearing you up inside."

"Yeah, Ms. Martínez. That's how I feel. All torn up inside. I hate myself and I hate my mom, too."

"Maya, those are all normal feelings that you're having. You're going through some rough changes in your life right now. So is your mom."

"Well, I just want things to be like they were before," Maya said, releasing a few more tears.

I handed her another Kleenex, wishing that there were some magical way I could make her pain disappear. But I knew it would take time, a great deal of time.

"Maya," I said, gently. "I really think you should go back home and give your mom another chance. Your mom loves you very much. I know it's hard to believe, but she's hurting inside just as much as you are."

"Yeah, I guess so. I just feel so angry at her."

"I know you do. But don't you think it's better to go home and talk to her, tell her exactly how you're feeling?"

Maya was silent for a moment. I knew she was desperately trying to sort out her feelings for Sonia. Poor Sonia. She was probably going out of her mind with worry by now.

"I'll go with you if you want, Maya," I added, hoping she would agree with me.

"Do you really think I should go home, Ms. Martínez?" Maya asked hesitatingly.

"Yes, I do, Maya. I know how much your mom loves you. I think you both need to sit down and talk to each other."

"Yeah, I guess so. But I'm scared. What if she's so mad that she won't let me come home?"

"Let's not worry about something that may not even happen, okay? Anyway, I'll be right there next to you."

Maya's face was starting to relax. "Thanks, Ms. Martínez."

"Shrinks aren't so bad after all, right, Maya?" I said, teasing.

This time Maya revealed a half-smile and I knew that she was already starting to feel better.

✎ ✐ ✎

As I pulled up in front of Sonia's house, I couldn't help but notice how the neighborhood Maya lived in contrasted with Juanita's. Both sides of the street were lined with perfectly designed bi-level homes with perfect lawns. This was definitely not the *barrio*. According to Sonia, there were few if any people of color in this area.

I reached over and patted Maya gently on the hand before we both got out of the car. "Everything is going to work out," I whispered to her as we approached the front steps.

As soon as Maya opened the front door, Sonia appeared looking nervous and tired. *"M'ija,"* Sonia gasped. Where have you been? I've been calling everywhere trying to find out where you went."

Maya stared at Sonia, and for a moment I questioned whether I should intercede or keep quiet.

"I'm so sorry, Mom," Maya finally whispered.

"I'm sorry, too, *m'ija,"* Sonia said. "I'm just glad you're home." Then, all of a sudden, they were both crying and hugging each other while I watched in relief.

✎   ✐   ✐

The next morning I received a call from Sonia thanking me again and telling me that for the first time she and Maya had been able to talk frankly about the divorce without getting into an argument. Sonia had even revealed to Maya that she was seeing a therapist to help her cope with her feelings about the divorce. Maya's reaction to Sonia's news had been positive, and she had in turn told Sonia about her appointment with me on Monday.

Before we hung up, I reminded Sonia that it would take time for Maya to readjust and for both of them to re-structure their relationship. Sonia always expected things to happen right away. Now she would have to learn to be patient.

TWELVE
Ms. Martínez

On Monday afternoon, I was finishing up the paperwork on my three o'clock appointment when the buzzer from the front desk rang, letting me know that my next patient had arrived. I hurried out to the reception area eager to see Maya. I felt a sense of relief when I saw her standing in the reception area waiting for me. She was wearing a pair of faded blue-jeans with holes in the knees that reminded me of when I was a teenager.

"Hi, Ms. Martínez," Maya said. "I bet you thought I wouldn't come."

"Oh, I knew you wouldn't be able to pass up seeing what a shrink's office looks like," I said, smiling.

Maya's face broke out in a smile.

"Follow me to my think tank," I ordered.

As soon as we were inside my office, Maya proceeded to lie down on the leather couch, stretching out her lanky body. "Okay, doc," she teased. "I'm ready."

I started to laugh. No wonder Juanita admired Maya as much as she did. Maya was one of a kind.

"So this is what a shrink's office looks like," Maya exclaimed, sitting back up.

"Quite an exciting place," I replied, feeling amused by Maya's forceful personality. She was a lot like Sonia, even though neither would ever admit it.

"What you need are some cool posters," Maya advised me. "Like one of Onyx or maybe Lighter Shade of Brown."

"You're probably right, Maya. That would certainly add some color to the dull walls. Maybe sometime you can help me pick some out."

"That would be cool," Maya said, crossing her skinny legs.

The room suddenly filled with silence. I started to feel a slight tension forming between Maya and myself. Finally, Maya spoke up. "My mom and I made up after you left."

"That's great, Maya."

"Yeah, I guess so. We talked about the divorce, too." A sad look appeared on Maya's face. "I guess I just don't understand why it had to happen to us. When I went to school in the Bay Area, I was always so proud because I was the only one whose parents weren't divorced."

"Divorce can happen to anyone, Maya. It's not something that's planned," I said in a gentle voice.

"My grandma said only *gringos* got divorced," Maya blurted out.

I had to smile at her. "Of course not. It even happens to people like me."

Maya's eyes widened and she looked at me in disbelief. "You were divorced, Ms. Martínez?"

"Yes, Maya. A long, long time ago."

"Oh, I didn't know. My mom never told me."

"I was very young like your mom when I married for the first time, and, to make a long story short, it didn't work out." I hoped that I wasn't sounding too flippant about the whole thing.

Maya was gazing out the window now. "I really miss my dad," she whispered. "It's so lonely without him." A few tears started to roll down her cheeks, but she quickly brushed them away with the back of her hand.

"I know how much you must miss your dad. Has he come to visit you yet?"

"No, he hasn't. And every time I call him, he says he's very busy and doesn't know when he can come see me. Sometimes I think he's just making excuses, that he really doesn't want to see me."

Now the tears were streaming down Maya's face. I reached over and handed her a Kleenex. "I'm sure your dad loves you, Maya. Divorce is a painful thing for everyone, and sometimes men have a more difficult time adjusting."

"I don't blame my dad," Maya continued in a sad voice. "It's all my mom's fault anyway. Grandma thinks so, too."

"And why do you feel it's all your mom's fault?" I asked, remembering my own mother's reaction when I had finally left Raúl.

"Mom's the one who kicked him out. She's the one who told him to leave. I heard her tell him that night."

"I see. Have you asked your mom about this? Have you asked her to explain why she asked him to leave?"

"No, I guess not," Maya answered, frowning. "We talked about the divorce a little, but not about why she told him to leave. But Grandma said it was Mom's fault. She said if my mom hadn't been

so busy getting an education, she wouldn't have
ignored my dad and maybe he wouldn't have left."

This all sounded so familiar. I felt as if I were
hearing my mother's own voice from years back:
"Sandra, why do you have to get a Ph.D.? Why
can't you just be satisfied with being married and
having kids?" Poor Sonia. I knew exactly how she
was feeling. All that guilt. Why was it that women
in Mexican and Chicano cultures were not supposed to have a profession? I only hoped Maya was
smart enough to reject all these old-fashioned
beliefs.

Maya was staring at me, waiting for my
response. "Maya," I began slowly. "Don't you think
you need to give your mom a chance to explain?
After all, it takes two people to make or break a
relationship. Aren't you proud of your mom for getting an education?"

"Yeah, I guess so. I just feel so confused that I
don't know what to think anymore." Maya's eyes
were filling with tears again, and I reached over
and patted her hand. "But last night we talked. I
told her how lonely I've felt ever since Dad left,
how I hate coming home."

"And what did your mom say?"

"She told me she felt lonely, too. That surprised me a lot. I thought she was happy Dad left."

"I think your mom is probably just as broken
up inside as you are, Maya," I said reassuringly.

"That's exactly how I feel, Ms. Martínez. All
broken up into little pieces."

Maya was crying again. I handed her some
more Kleenex and waited for her to calm down.
After a few minutes, I spoke to her. "Things will get
better, Maya. Trust me. The important thing is

that you've taken the first step and you're talking about your feelings and not keeping them all bottled up inside."

"Yeah, I guess so," Maya said, revealing a faint smile. "I already feel better just talking to you, Ms. Martínez."

"I'm glad. And I know there are many people around you who love you and care about you—Juanita, your mom. And give your dad some time to adjust. He'll come around. Don't close the door on him. Keep calling him, and before long he'll be able to talk with you about everything."

There was a glimmer of hope in Maya's eyes. "You really think so, Ms. Martínez?"

"Yes, I do. Just be patient. And now it's time for my next appointment. How about if we meet at this same time next week?"

"Sure, Ms. Martínez. I'd really like that," Maya answered hopefully.

When I said goodbye to Maya at the door, I noticed that her eyes were shining again and she seemed more at ease. I couldn't help but feel pleased with myself. It would take some time and hard work, but Maya would survive. So would Sonia. After all, weren't women of color the greatest survivors?

THIRTEEN
Maya

I think a lot about what Ms. Martínez said to me. One evening, I decide to take her advice. My mom and I are in the family room watching "Jeopardy" when I blurt out the question that has been bothering me. "Mom, why did you tell Dad to leave?"

A surprised look appears on Mom's face, and in a slow quivering voice, she answers, "I know it will be hard for you to understand, Maya, but the love your dad and I once felt for each other disappeared a long time ago. For quite some time now, your dad and I had been living separate lives. Your dad was unhappy and so was I, but we both kept avoiding the problem and, well, it got to the point where I just couldn't let it go on like this anymore. One of us had to make the decision, so I asked him to leave. He always hated Laguna from the first day we moved here, and so he decided to move back to the Bay Area."

Mom puts her head down, but not before I notice the tears in her eyes. Even then I can't seem to feel sorry for her. "So you kicked him out, just like that?" I say defensively, wiping away the tears that are trickling down my cheeks. When Mom finally looks up at me, I know that my words have hurt her. Why is it that I want to hurt her?

"No, *m'ija*," she insists, wiping a tear from her eyes. "It wasn't like that. We both agreed it would be better for your dad to live somewhere else. I'm happy here at the university, you seemed happy at Roosevelt, so we both thought it would be better this way."

"But why didn't you tell me he was leaving? Why didn't you both talk to me about it?" I ask accusingly.

"I'm sorry, Maya. We screwed up. I guess we didn't want to hurt you. We thought the less we told you the better."

"You should have told me!" I shout back, getting up from the couch. This time I don't give Mom a chance to respond. I race back to my room, slamming the door behind me.

Later that night I can hear Mom's muffled sobs coming from the bathroom. I start to feel guilty. I don't know why I have to be so mean to her. At least she told me the truth about Dad. At least now I know.

The next day at school I realize that I am finally starting to pay attention in my classes. I even jot down the homework assignments, thinking maybe I can bring my grades back up. I don't know why, but I'm starting to feel like myself again.

At lunchtime, I'm reaching inside my locker for my lunch bag when Juanita comes over to talk to me. "Hi, Maya," she says.

"Oh, hi, Johnny," I answer, slamming my locker door shut.

"Did you and your mom make up?" Juanita asks.

"Yeah, sort of. We talked a lot. Thanks for everything, Johnny."

Juanita's face breaks into a smile. "Wanna eat lunch with us today?" she asks me hopefully. I remember how Dad used to tease her about her two big dimples, telling her that she had two large holes in her face.

"Yeah, sure," I answer, trying to put Dad's image out of my mind.

We walk together out of the building toward the parking lot. I'm getting ready to tell Juanita about my meeting with Ms. Martínez when I feel someone pulling me from behind. All of a sudden Shane is standing in front of me. "Hey, Maya," he says. "We're waiting for you. Come on."

I notice the tense look that has appeared on Juanita's face. "Oh, hi, Shane," I mutter. "I think I'll eat with Johnny today." I am starting to feel very nervous. I know that Shane is used to getting his way.

"Excuse us for a minute, Johnny," Shane says, pulling me firmly by the arm to his side. "Don't be stupid, Maya. You're eating with me," Shane orders me, tightening his grip on my arm.

"Let go of me, Shane," I tell him in an angry voice. "You're hurting me."

"You go where I go, babe," Shane insists, pulling me closer to him.

My arm hurts. I start to feel scared, wondering what I should do next, when a familiar voice comes to my rescue.

"Let her go, Shane," Tyrone growls.

I turn sideways to look at Tyrone. Tommy and Rudy are standing next to him. Suddenly Shane lets go of my arm and glares at Tyrone. "Stay out of this, punk," Shane says in a threatening tone. "This isn't any of your business."

"Shut up, Shane," Tyrone answers. "I don't want any trouble."

The next thing I know, Shane moves closer to Tyrone and pushes him real hard on the chest. "Stop it," I yell, placing myself between Shane and Tyrone.

Rudy and Tommy quickly grab Tyrone by the arm and hold him back. After what happened to Juanita last year, I don't want Tyrone to get kicked out of school for fighting.

"Everything is cool, Ty," I lie. "I was planning on eating with Shane and Charley today."

Tyrone is looking straight at me. I can see the anger in his eyes. "Are you sure you wanna go eat with them, Maya?" Juanita asks me.

I know that my words will hurt Tyrone, but I'll do anything to avoid a fight. "Yeah, I'm sure," I answer, grabbing Shane by the arm. "See you, Johnny."

As we start to walk away, Shane flips Tyrone off and Rudy yells something back at him. I quicken my step so that we can get away from Tyrone before anything else can happen.

I don't say anything to Shane until we get in the back seat of Charley's car. "Shane, why do you have to act like that?" I ask, feeling humiliated and angry.

"You're my babe now," Shane replies, putting his arm around me. When Charley lets out a laugh from the front seat, I feel like crying because I know that I don't belong here. I hate Charley. I hate cigarette smoke, and I hate heavy-metal music.

Later that evening I'm lying in bed wide awake when I feel the sudden urge to talk to my dad. I reach for the phone and dial his number. It rings for a long time and I'm about to give up when he finally picks up the receiver.

"Hello."

"Hi, Dad. It's me, Maya."

"Maya, what are you doing calling this late?" my father asks in a scolding voice.

"I'm sorry, Dad. I know it's late, but you're never home when I call, and I need to talk to you."

"Well," my dad sighs, "I've been working long hours and by the time I get home, it's late. But I've been meaning to call you. Your mom told me about everything that's been going on."

There is a long, awkward pause. All of a sudden, I am embarrassed. I can imagine what Dad must think of me now.

"Maya, are you still there?" he asks calmly.

"Yeah," I manage to mutter. "But why don't you ever call me?" For a moment I imagine Dad's handsome face, the dimple on his chin, the wrinkles that appear across his forehead when he is worried. I feel like I am about to cry. I miss him so much.

"Maya, I know I haven't been a very good father lately, but things have been rough for me, too." I can hear Dad's voice start to crack as if he is about to cry. I've only seen Dad cry once in his life. That was on the day we buried Grandpa.

"*Flaca*, I want you to come up on the train for Thanksgiving. I already mentioned it to your mom. Would you like that? My apartment is small, but I think you'll like it. What do you say, *Flaca*?"

It makes me feel good to hear Dad call me "skinny" in Spanish again. Ever since I was a little girl, he's called me that. "Yeah, I'd really like that, Dad," I answer. "Because I really miss you."

"I know you do, *Flaca*. Maybe when you come we can have a good talk about everything that's been happening."

"Yeah, I'd like that, too."

"Okay. It's all set then. I'll call you in a few weeks to make the arrangements. And, *Flaca*..."

"Yeah, Dad?"

"I miss you, too."

When I hang up the receiver, I feel happy inside. Maybe Ms. Martínez is right. Things will get better.

FOURTEEN
Maya

By the time Friday arrives, I'm relieved that I won't have to see Shane and Charley for a few days. All week long I've felt pressured into eating with them at lunchtime. I know this hurts Tyrone's feelings, but I don't want him to get into a fight with Shane on account of me. After all, I was the one who dumped him for Shane.

As soon as I get home from school, I kick off my shoes and sit down to watch the last half of "Oprah." Today's show is on smoking and the high number of teenagers who smoke. I think about Shane and Charley and how they always seem to have a cigarette in their hands. I'm glad I don't smoke. Mom always says smoking is bad for your health. I guess she's right. I guess Mom isn't such a bad person after all.

The show is about to end when the telephone rings. I'm surprised to hear Mom's voice on the other line. *"M'ija,"* she says in a rushed voice. "I forgot that I have to attend a lecture given by a faculty member that we're thinking of hiring. There's a reception afterwards, so I won't be home until about seven. There's frozen pizza in the fridge. Will you be okay? I bet you're watching 'Oprah.'"

"Yeah, but it's almost over," I answer, smiling to myself. Mom loves to watch "Oprah," especially on Fridays when she usually gets home early. She says watching "Oprah" relaxes her after a stressful day on campus.

"Well, don't veg all afternoon. Read something. And I'll be home just as soon as I can."

"Don't worry, Mom. I'll be fine."

"Okay, *m'ija*. Have to go now. See you at seven."

I hang up the receiver and lay back down on the couch so I can watch the end of "Oprah." I close my eyes and before I know it I've drifted off to sleep. When I awaken, it is almost five o'clock. My stomach starts to growl, so I turn of the television and head for the kitchen. I pop the pizza in the oven and sit down at the table with a can of Pepsi to read my new issue of *Seventeen* magazine.

Half an hour later, I'm taking the pizza out of the oven when the door bell rings. I open the front door and Shane and Charley force themselves into the entryway. I am so stunned that I don't say a word as they walk past me into the family room.

"Hey, *esa*," Charley says, walking over to my mom's stereo. "This is some kind of house."

I am finally able to speak. "Shane," I say following after them. "What are you doing here? I'm not allowed to have friends over when my mom isn't home."

"Relax, babe," Shane answers as he sits on the couch and starts to play around with the television remote control.

"Your old lady sure has some kinda record collection," Charley tells me.

I can feel the tension running up and down my back. "Leave those alone," I holler. "My mom hates it when someone messes with her albums."

"Cool it, *esa*. I'm only looking," Charley says as he flips through the albums on the record case.

The room suddenly fills with blaring music from MTV. I'm so angry that I walk over to Shane and grab the remote control from his hand and turn the power off. Shane lets out a sarcastic laugh, saying, "Don't be so uptight, Maya. Your mom won't find out we were here."

I feel a sudden panic. I can't believe this is actually happening. "Come on, Shane," I beg. "Please leave."

Instead of listening to my pleas, Shane grabs me by the arm and pulls me down on the couch next to him. "I miss you, babe," he whispers, putting his arms around me.

I manage to struggle free of him. "Stop it, Shane," I yell, getting up and moving away from him. All of a sudden I notice that Charley has disappeared from the room. I'm about to go look for him when he reappears, waving a bottle of vodka and two glasses. "Look what I found," he tells Shane.

"Put those away!" I explode.

Charley doesn't listen to me. Instead, he hands Shane the bottle of liquor. "Just a little drink and then we'll go," Shane says, opening the bottle.

I stare in disbelief as Shane sets the glasses on the coffee table and pours some vodka into them. My body feels frozen. I'm not sure what I should do next. Maybe if I let them have one drink, they'll leave.

"You promise you'll leave after one drink?" I finally whisper.

"Yeah. Don't sweat it, Maya," Shane says, handing Charley one of the glasses.

After Shane empties his glass, he fills it with more vodka and comes over to where I'm standing. "Come on, babe. It's your turn," he orders, holding the glass up to my lips.

"Stop it, Shane," I holler, pushing the glass away from me.

"Come on, Maya," Charley insists. "Don't be a chicken."

"Come on, babe. Just one drink and I promise you we'll leave," Shane says, holding the glass up to my mouth.

I know that I am trapped. I know that Shane won't leave me alone until I do what he asks. I take the glass from him and pretend to take a small drink. Then I tell them both, "Get out or I'll call the police."

"Yeah, let's go," Shane tells Charley. "Maya must be on the rag today."

I lock the door as soon as they leave. Then I hurriedly pick up the empty glasses and the bottle of vodka. I pour some water into the vodka bottle so that it looks as if no one has tampered with it. Then I put the bottle back in the same spot in the kitchen cabinet where my mom had it.

✎ ✏ ✎

Later that evening, when Mom comes home and asks me how everything went, I lie and tell her everything was fine. I feel miserable again because

I hate lying to her. Then I start to wonder what I ever saw in Shane in the first place.

FIFTEEN
Ms. Martínez

"Wake up, hon," Frank said, tapping me lightly on the shoulder.

As usual, Frank was wide awake and full of energy. Not me. I detested Monday mornings. I forced my eyes open and slowly turned myself around. I had to smile. Frank was standing there in his yuppie-looking shirt and tie, holding a cup of espresso and a blueberry muffin. "You really spoil me, Frank," I told him.

"Yes, hon, I don't know what you'd do without me," Frank teased as he handed me my breakfast. "Now give me a kiss because I have to go earn some *dinero*."

I laughed at Frank's Spanish pronunciation. Then I leaned forward to let him kiss me on the lips. As he disappeared through the bedroom door, Frank blew me another and reminded me, "Don't forget how much your hunk of burning love loves you!"

Frank was such a clown. But he was absolutely right. Without him, my life would be dull and humorless. Yet, how he could be in such a good mood so early in the morning was beyond me. I was definitely not a morning person. If I could, I'd sleep late every morning, just as I had done during the summer when I took a month off. It had been wonderful. Now I didn't feel quite as burned-out as before, and I actually looked forward to seeing my clients again.

I was about to take the last bite of my blueberry muffin when the telephone rang. I hesitated before picking up the receiver. The only person who ever called me this early in the morning was my mother. "Hello," I finally answered.

"Hello, Sandra," my mother's voice greeted me.

"Oh, hello, Mom," I answered, trying my best not to sound irritated. I knew that every time my mother called this early in the morning it meant trouble. "Is everything okay, Mom?" I asked point-blank. Is Dad all right?"

"Yes, your father's fine. We're both fine."

I could tell by the tension in her voice that something was definitely wrong. Why didn't she just spit it out? "Well, what's up? Why are you calling so early?"

There was silence on the line, but after a minute or two, my mother finally spoke, "Raúl is dead, Sandra."

I felt the blood rush to my head. "What?" I gasped.

"Raúl died last night. I thought you should know."

My heart was beating faster and I felt a dull ache forming somewhere deep inside. Raúl dead. The words just didn't seem to register in my mind. "Are you sure, Mom?" I asked.

"Yes, Sandra. My *comadre* Martina told me."

My eyes started to fill with tears while images of Raúl raced through my mind. Raúl.

"Sandra, are you okay?" my mom asked, gently.

"Yes, Mom. I'm okay. How did it happen?"

"Well, you know he drank all the time. I guess they found him dead. He had choked sometime during the night. I guess he was drinking hard liquor. That's what my *comadre* said."

"That's so sad, Mom," I whispered. "Didn't he have a couple of kids?"

"Yes, he had a boy and a girl. I guess his wife left him a long time ago on account of his drinking. The funeral is on Saturday. I think you should come."

It was just like my mother, telling me what I should do. But this time I had to agree with her. "Yes, I think I should too," I answered slowly.

"Well, that's all I wanted to tell you. Call and let us know what day you're coming, okay, *hija* ?"

"Yes, Mom, I will," I reassured her, slowly hanging up the receiver.

As I laid back down against the pillow, Raúl's handsome young face appeared before me. And suddenly, I found myself crying, crying for those memories buried deep inside of me.

Back at my office, I managed to get through all my morning appointments without letting anyone know I was mourning Raúl's death. Listening to my clients' endless problems allowed me to push it temporarily out of my mind. But by the time my afternoon appointment with Maya came, I was drained from the day's emotions.

When I walked out to the reception area, I found Maya sitting down, fidgeting with her nails.

It was obvious that she was feeling nervous that day.

"Hello, Maya," I greeted her, trying to sound as cheerful as possible. "Follow me to the back."

"Sure, Ms. Martínez," Maya said, following me down the hallway to my office.

Unlike our first session, Maya was quiet and tense as she sat down on the couch across from me. "Well, young lady," I began, "how have things been going between you and your mom?"

Maya shrugged. "I guess you can say a lot better. I took your advice and asked her why she kicked my dad out."

"You did?"

"Yeah. My mom explained it all to me, but I still can't understand how two people can stop loving each other just like that." Maya's eyes clouded with sadness and I knew that the divorce was hurting her deeply.

"I know it's difficult to understand, Maya. But people do grow apart, especially when they marry very young."

"Is that why you got divorced, too, Ms. Martínez?" Maya asked, staring straight at me.

I knew that I needed to be honest with her, but how could I possibly explain about my marriage to Raúl, especially today. For a moment I felt as if Maya were the therapist and I were her patient. "Yes, Maya," I answered, running my hand through my hair. "That was one of the main reasons. We were both very young."

"Well, I still don't understand why it had to happen to my parents," Maya mumbled, bowing her head.

"I know how you feel, Maya. Divorce is very painful and it takes time to accept." The room filled with silence as I thought about Raúl's sudden death and the marriage we once had.

"I talked to my dad the other day," Maya suddenly blurted out.

"That's great," I said, forcing myself back to the present and away from Raúl.

"Yeah. He even invited me up for Thanksgiving. He also told me he was sorry he hasn't called me."

"I'm so glad, Maya. And how do you feel about going to visit him?"

"It'll be different, I guess. Mom said I can take the train up. And Dad said he'd take me out to eat at some fancy restaurant."

"That sounds like fun. San Francisco is a beautiful city."

Maya was quiet again. I waited patiently for her to begin speaking, but when she didn't say anything, I broke the silence. "How are things at school?"

Now Maya was frowning. "Not so good," she answered, folding her arms tightly across her waist.

"Why is that?"

"Well, I'm doing better in my classes, but I'm sort of having problems with some of my friends."

"What kind of problems," I asked, gently.

"Well," Maya hesitated. "Do you remember my friends, Shane and Charley, the ones my mom hates? Well, the other day Johnny wanted me to eat lunch with her and the other guys, like I used to, and Shane got upset. He almost punched Tyrone out."

"And how did you react to that?"

"I was so embarrassed. I didn't know what to do. I wanted to go with Johnny, but I didn't want a fight to break out. I was kind of scared after what happened last year to Johnny. So I decided to go eat with Shane and Charley."

"I'm glad a fight didn't break out."

"Yeah, me too, but Shane is really bugging me. He's acting real possessive."

"How is he acting possessive?" I asked cautiously.

"Well, he thinks I should only be with him and Charley at lunch time. And then last Friday night when my mom wasn't home, he showed up at my house with Charley. I told them to leave, but they wouldn't. And they even got into a bottle of vodka my mom had in the kitchen."

"Did you tell your mom about this?"

"No, I was afraid," Maya said, frowning. "But I'm really getting sick of Shane's attitude."

"Why is that?"

"I don't know, Ms. Martínez. At first it was really exciting being with Shane, cruising around San Martin. But now it just seems like Shane and Charley are disrespectful to everyone. I don't think I want to hang out with them anymore."

"Then why are you still doing it?"

"I guess I'm afraid to tell Shane no. I'm afraid of what might happen."

"Maya, the only way to change something you don't feel good about is to confront the problem. And yes, you're right. It can be scary, but you're the only one who can change the situation."

"Yeah, you're right, Ms. Martínez. I guess I'm just scared."

"Maya, let's try something. Let's pretend that Shane is here right now and you want to have lunch with Juanita, but he wants you to go with him and Charley. What could you say to make him get the point?"

Maya was quiet for a moment as she searched for the right words. After a few minutes, she said, "Well, I guess I could say, 'Shane, I don't want to hang out with you and Charley anymore. Please leave me alone.'"

"Good girl, Maya. It's important to be direct and get your message across loud and clear. Also, when you confront Shane, try to do it when there are other people around. That way you have someone to turn to for help if there's a problem." I glanced quickly at my watch. "Looks like we're out of time, Maya. Now, will you think carefully about everything we've discussed today?"

"Yeah, I will, Ms. Martínez," Maya answered, standing up.

"Good girl," I said, reaching over and giving her a big hug before she disappeared out of my office.

SIXTEEN
Ms. Martínez

When I told Frank I wanted to attend Raúl's funeral, he was very sympathetic and understanding. He even offered to drive me to Delano. But I knew that things were very busy for him at the accounting office where he worked, so I insisted on going alone. That evening I called my mother to let her know I would arrive on Friday and stay only until the funeral on Saturday. As usual, she didn't approve of my plans and insisted that I spend the whole weekend there, but I was firm about my plans. One day and night were all that I could stand being back home with my parents.

The four-hour drive from Laguna to Delano was hot and depressing. As I drove through the San Joaquín Valley, passing field after field of crops and vineyards, I couldn't help but think about Juanita's family and all the other migrant workers who did stoop labor to support their families. I knew that if it hadn't been for the United Farm Worker's Union, farm workers today would not have such basic necessities as portable toilets in the fields. Yet, the life of the migrant worker hadn't changed that much. Every now and then the local newspapers were filled with horror stories about farmers who abused their workers. And then the pesticide poisoning, all those children born with deformities. How ironic that California was one of the wealthiest states and yet, here in these fields, were the poorest people.

When I finally pulled into Delano, I felt a sense of excitement. In this small, virtually unknown town, history had been made. It was here that César Chávez had lived and organized the UFW. I thought back to my last visit to Delano for César's funeral. Delano was filled with thousands of people. I hadn't seen Delano filled with so many people since the grape boycott of 1965.

Sonia and I had driven over for the night of the final rosary, which was held at Forty Acres, the UFW's original headquarters located several miles outside of Delano. Large tents had been set up to accommodate César's family and the public. Camera crews surrounded the tents, waiting for the dignitaries to arrive, and the air was filled with the sound of helicopters. One of Sonia's former students, who was working for the UFW, had given us seats in the V.I.P. section.

A large altar had been placed at the front of the tents for the more than twenty priests who officiated at the rosary and funeral mass. A portrait of César stood to the right of the altar, and to the left was a huge portrait of the Virgin of Guadalupe. The UFW flag was hanging in the background and there were small UFW banners all around the tents. When César's casket was carried in, it was placed next to his portrait. It was a simple pine casket. César had wished to be buried in a home-made casket like the one his brother had made years ago to bury farm workers who couldn't afford their own caskets.

As long as I live, I will never forget the throngs of people of all ages and colors who lined up for hours throughout the night of the final rosary to say goodbye to their great leader. It was one of the most exciting but sad moments in my life being there among, not only the humble farm workers, but the famous people, such as Coretta King, Jesse Jackson, the Kennedys, and the well-known Latino actors who came to honor the memory of César Chávez. The night was filled with shouts of *¡Qué viva César Chávez! ¡Qué viva Dolores Huerta! ¡Qué viva La Unión de Campesinos!* On the morning of the funeral, we all gathered as we had done in 1965 for the final march with César from Forty Acres to downtown and back to the funeral mass.

And now, driving along Main Street, Delano didn't seem like the same place without César Chávez. It was empty now, devoid of the magic.

As I turned into the street where my parents lived, I spotted Don Anselmo's junked pick-up truck next to my parents' house. Ever since I could remember, that old green truck had been parked there. When I was little, my friends and I would use it to play hide and seek.

I pulled into the driveway and as soon as I opened the car door, my mother appeared on the front steps of the old familiar house. She never seemed to change: the same cotton dress with an apron pulled tightly over it, the same hairstyle, the same worn-out gray shoes. *"M'ija,"* she greeted me, drying her hands on her apron. *"Llegaste temprano."*

"Hello, mom," I said, embracing her. "It seemed to take forever."

"*Qué flaca estás, hija.* I'm making your favorite for dinner, enchiladas."

I smiled as I followed my mother inside the small kitchen. She knew how much I loved enchiladas and she never missed an opportunity to try and fatten me up.

When we walked into the living room, I found my father sitting in his old brown recliner watching the afternoon news. He looked older now. There was more grey in his thin black hair and his face was red and puffy. I walked over to him and gave him a quick hug.

"How was the drive?" he asked.

"Oh, not too bad. Anything good on the news?" I asked, sitting next to him on the couch.

"No, just the usual murders," he replied. Then he was silent, like always.

I gazed at the familiar photographs that covered the walls: my high school graduation picture, my *Tía* Luisa's family portrait, a picture of my grandparents' wedding day. I froze when I came to my brother Andy's picture. It was the last picture taken of him in high school. I felt a dull ache as I remembered the car accident and how the police said he had taken his own life. Although many years had passed since then, it still felt like yesterday.

I was relieved when my mother came into the living room and suggested I lie down to rest for a while. I hurried into my old bedroom, hoping to forget about Andy's death.

When I woke up from my nap, I showered and went outside to join my father in the back yard. He

showed me the small garden he had planted and
we picked some cucumbers for dinner. Then we sat
and visited for a while. He talked about how much
Delano was growing and about the new houses that
were being built on the south side of town. Then he
asked how Frank was doing. My father had always
liked Frank, and I knew he was sorry Frank hadn't
been able to come with me.

After dinner we all went back into the living
room to watch television. My father was a stickler
for his routine: first the six o'clock news, then old
reruns of his favorite show, "Three's Company."
Then we watched an old Antonio Aguilar movie on
the local Spanish channel. My dad loved Antonio
Aguilar. He collected all his albums and even had
some copies of his old movies. As soon as the movie
ended, we watched the local news. By 11 o'clock we
were ready for bed.

On Sunday morning my mother and I drove to
St. John's Catholic Church for Raúl's funeral service. When we arrived, the church was already full,
but we managed to find a place next to Don
Anselmo and his wife. As I looked around, I recog-
nized some of my parents' friends, but none of the
young faces looked familiar.

The funeral service was touching. My eyes
filled with tears as I watched Raúl's parents and
his widow with their two children march solemnly
up the church aisle behind the casket. Father Steve
described death as a passage to a new and better
life that awaits each of us. I thought of Andy again,
hoping that God had forgiven him for taking his
own life.

At the cemetery, I cried as Raúl's casket was
lowered to the ground. My mother squeezed my

hand gently, letting me know that she understood my sadness. Then we walked over to give our condolences to Raúl's family. When Raúl's mother saw me, she embraced me, whispering, *"Gracias por venir, hija."* As I shook Raúl's wife's hand, I couldn't help but notice how much the young boy sitting next to her resembled Raúl.

After the funeral we drove back to the house so that I could get ready for my return trip to Laguna. I knew that my mother was upset because I wasn't joining her and Dad for the customary meal after the funeral at Raúl's parents' house, but I had begged off, insisting that Frank expected me for dinner. I knew this would convince my mother, since she firmly believed a woman must tend to her husband's needs before anything else.

As I drove back home to Laguna, Raúl's son's face kept flashing in my mind, and all of a sudden, I found myself remembering the unexpected pregnancy. Raúl had never known. I had discovered I was pregnant right after we had separated for the final time, but I was determined to get away from Raúl's cycle of self-destruction. I never told anyone about the pregnancy, not even my own mother. Only my *Tía* Lola had known about it. And later, when I miscarried, I was relieved it was all over. But I was left with a deep dark secret that would haunt me the rest of my life.

SEVENTEEN
Maya

"The train's coming," I tell Mom, trying my best to sound as grown up as possible even though I'm scared. I have never traveled anywhere by myself, and it's exciting but scary at the same time.

As the train comes to a complete stop, Mom reminds me for the hundredth time, "And don't forget, call me as soon as you get to your dad's apartment."

"Don't worry, Mom. I will," I tell her, picking up my suitcase. I can tell that she's just as nervous as I am about this trip.

"Well, *m'ija*, I guess you better board," she says reluctantly.

"Okay, Mom. I'll see you in a few days. Love you." I kiss her lightly on the cheek. Then I quickly climb the steps onto the train and take the first empty seat I see.

As the train starts to pull away, I wave. I can't help but notice the sad look on Mom's face. I keep right on waving until she is no longer in sight. Then all of a sudden I find myself wishing she were with me. As I look around, I see faces belonging to people I've never seen before. I start to wonder what I'm doing here all alone, but then I remember that Dad is waiting for me. It's been almost five months since I last saw him. I wonder if he still has a beard? I wonder if he'll recognize me when he sees me?

I spend the first hour of the trip reading from my *Seventeen* magazine and eating the snacks that Mom packed for me. I start to feel sleepy and make the seat recline so I can take a nap. When I wake up, the train is passing through Salinas. I can feel a tightening in my stomach. I know that in another hour I'll see my dad. I can't imagine what we'll say to each other. Everything is so different now.

When the train pulls into the San Jose train station, I nervously run a comb through my long, stringy hair. Then I gather my things together and head for the nearest exit. As I get off the train and onto the platform, I look around for Dad, but I don't see him. I start to feel panicky, wondering if he's forgotten to pick me up. Then I suddenly hear Dad call out my name. He is standing behind a group of people. I hurry over to meet him as he pushes his way through the crowd.

"You've gotten taller, *flaca*," he tells me, putting his arms around me and kissing me.

I remember what it feels like to be safe and secure in Dad's strong arms. When he lets go of me, I stare up at him, and exclaim, "Dad, you shaved your beard. And your *panza* looks smaller," I add, staring at his belly.

Dad lets out a loud, resounding laugh. "It's all that work. I never have time to eat. And my beard was itching a lot so I decided to shave it."

He takes my suitcase and I follow him to the parking lot. We pass several rows of cars until he finally stops in front of a shiny black Porsche. "How do you like my new car?" Dad asks exuberantly.

I let out a squeal of joy. "Cool! When are you going to let me drive it, Dad?" I ask.

Dad ignores my question and unlocks the doors. As he starts the car, I still can't believe I'm actually riding in a brand-new Porsche. I can hardly wait to tell all my friends.

After we are on the freeway headed for San Francisco, Dad asks me about school. I tell him that I'm doing better and hope to bring my grades up by second semester. He seems pleased, and I'm relieved that he doesn't lecture me on the way I've been acting. When I ask him about his new job, he tells me that he's a manager in an engineering department and that he likes it a lot, but that he has to work long hours. Then we're both quiet as I gaze out the window at all the buildings and companies that make up the Silicon Valley. All of a sudden, I feel homesick for the volcanic peaks of Laguna.

An hour later, we arrive in San Francisco. It is such a beautiful city with its tall buildings and fish-smelling air. It's so different from Laguna. There are people of all ethnic backgrounds scurrying around. When I ask my dad if he likes living here, he answers, "Yes, Maya, I do. You're the only thing missing. I've always liked big cities. Not cow country, like your mom. And I like the different types of people here."

When we get to the apartment complex where Dad lives, he parks the car underneath the building and we head for the second floor. As soon as we're inside his apartment, he takes me for a quick tour. First, he shows me the living room. It's fairly large and is connected to a small dining room that leads to a small, modern kitchen. Then he shows me the master bedroom and a smaller bedroom which he says will be mine whenever I visit. Finally, he shows me the bathroom we will share. I notice that the walls in his apartment are blank except for one in the living room where he has hung my high school picture from last year.

That night we order pizza and watch television. Dad tells me about his new friends that I'll be meeting tomorrow. He says we'll be eating at his friend Michelle's house in Marin County. Michelle works for the same company that he does. I wonder if she and Dad are dating, and I start to feel a little jealous. We stay up until almost two in the morning watching movies. Dad has always been a night owl. It used to drive Mom crazy.

On Thanksgiving day we drive over to Michelle's house. Michelle turns out to be sort of nice. She's kind of tall and has short auburn hair, but she's not as pretty as Mom. I meet two more of Dad's friends, Tim and Connie. Tim is an engineer, and his girlfriend Connie works at the Golden Gate Bridge. They're all very nice to me, but since I'm the youngest one there, I feel strange so I stick to Dad like glue. I can tell this bothers Michelle, but I really don't care.

Michelle and Connie have prepared a traditional Thanksgiving dinner. When we sit down to eat, I can't help but miss Mom. I wonder if she's eating all alone? Mom always makes tortillas for our Thanksgiving dinner. I wonder if she made some today. I barely touch my food, and Michelle teases me about being too skinny. I want to tell her to shut up, but I don't.

After dinner, Michelle insists we play "Yahtzee." I hate "Yahtzee," but I don't say anything. Then we all sit around and listen to music. Michelle likes classical music. On purpose, I ask if she has anything by Los Lobos. When she says "no" and asks me if they're from Spain, I start to laugh, but the look on Dad's face tells me to keep quiet.

At ten o'clock, I'm relieved when Dad finally says it's time to leave. After we say goodbye to Tim and Connie, Michelle walks us to the door. She makes a special point of telling me how much she enjoyed meeting me and that she hopes I'll come back again. I want to tell her that I'm really not interested, but I don't want to hurt Dad's feelings, so I tell her that would be nice.

On the way home, I ask Dad once more if Michelle is his new girlfriend, but he laughs and says she's only a good friend. I can't help but feel happy.

Friday turns out to be a fun day. My dad takes me to the theater to see a new comedy with Whoopi Goldberg. We pig out on popcorn and candy, just like in the old days. After the movie, Dad takes me to eat at his favorite hamburger joint in San Francisco—Mike's MegaBurger. Dad orders the biggest cheeseburger I have ever seen, and I tease him that his belly is going to return.

When we get back to the apartment, Dad lets me turn on his stereo and we sit down to listen to music. I am humming the verses to a song that I really like when he interrupts me.

"Maya. I guess now's a good time to talk. I want to discuss some things before you go back home."

"Yeah, sure," I answer, noticing the deep creases that have appeared across his forehead.

"Listen, *flaca*, I know you blame your mom for the divorce. But I think you should know that it was bound to happen sooner or later. Our marriage died a long time ago, but I just couldn't deal with the truth. Your mom was the one who had the guts to decide it was really over. I was angry about it, but she was right. We couldn't have gone on like that for much longer."

I can feel my eyes start to get watery. I quickly look away from Dad toward the patio door, suddenly feeling gray and foggy like the city.

"And I know I've been ignoring you, not calling you or anything, but I promise I'll do better now. It's just that, well, it's been rough for me being by myself, having to start all over again. It can be pretty damn scary to suddenly wake up and find yourself all alone."

The tears are streaming down my face now. I wipe them away with the back of my hand.

"And I missed you so much, Maya, that the thought of only being able to talk on the phone and not see you every day hurt too much. That's why I never called. I'm sorry if I hurt you, *Flaca*." Then he reaches over and puts his arms around me, holding me tight like he used to when I was a little girl.

"I miss you, too, Dad," I manage to whisper.

After a few minutes, Dad lets go of me and heads for the bathroom to get some Kleenex. I notice that his eyes are watery, too. When he comes back, he hands me a Kleenex, calling me a *mocosa*. We both laugh. Then he gives me another hug, telling me, "I love you, *Flaca*."

The next morning, when I say goodbye to Dad at the train station in San Jose, he promises to call me next week, and I promise to visit him as soon as I can. As the train pulls away, I realize that I feel better than I have in a long time. I can feel the empty space in my heart start to fill up again. Ms. Martínez was right. Dad really does love me.

EIGHTEEN
Maya

On Monday, it feels pretty good to be back in school, and I find myself trying harder in my classes. When I raise my hand in History class to answer a question about the Mexican-American War, I can tell that old Mrs. Clark is pleased. I want to tell her that my mom said the Southwest was stolen from Mexico and that it is really named *Aztlán*, but I decide not to. She probably wouldn't understand anyway.

At noon, I'm closing my locker when I feel someone tap me gently on the shoulder. I turn to find Juanita standing behind me. "Hi, Johnny," I say, smiling. "How was your Thanksgiving?"

"It was fun," Juanita answers. "My *Amá* cooked a turkey for the first time this year."

"Really? That's cool."

"How was your Thanksgiving?"

"It was fun, too. I went to my dad's in San Francisco. I saw his new apartment and met some of his friends."

"That's good, Maya," Juanita says, hesitating for a moment before continuing. "Do you want to eat lunch with us today?"

"Sure. Let's go," I answer right away.

Juanita stares at me in disbelief. "Come on, *¡Vámonos* !" I say, grabbing her by the arm.

As we head down the hallway, we hear Tommy call us from behind and we slow down to let him catch up with us."

"Hey, Maya, got anything good to eat today?" Tommy says, trying to grab my lunch bag out of my hand.

"Only *chile jalapeño*!" I tease back.

We walk out of the main building and head toward the football field. I'm feeling very happy about eating with my friends again when all of a sudden I spot Shane and Charley walking straight toward us. My stomach starts to feel all knotted up inside.

"*¡Híjole!*" Juanita groans.

"Don't sweat it, Maya," Tommy says.

Although I'm trying to act as if I haven't really noticed them, Shane moves over and stops right in front of me. "Hey, babe," he says, putting his hand on my arm. "I was looking for you."

Before I have time to say anything, Tommy answers for me, "Maya's eating with us today."

"Shut up," Shane says, glaring at Tommy. "I'm not talking to you." Then he turns to me and says, "You don't wanna eat with punks, do you, Maya?"

Charley starts laughing as Tommy's face turns bright red. Juanita moves closer to Tommy and grabs him by the arm, saying, "Don't pay attention to them, Tommy. They're nothing but jerks."

I can feel tiny beads of sweat forming on my nose, but all of a sudden, I know what I must do. I won't let anyone treat my friends like this. "Listen, Shane," I explode. "I don't want to hang out with you and Charley ever again. We're finished. Got it?

And if you don't lay off of me, my dad said he would come over here and personally give you the message."

Shane is about to grab me by the arm, but I don't give him the chance. I quickly take Juanita by the arm and start walking away from him.

"You bitch!" Shane hollers at me. "Who needs you anyway. There are plenty of other babes around."

As we walk further away from Shane and Charley, I burst into tears. Juanita puts her arms around me and Tommy tells me, "You did real good, Maya. I think he got the message."

I wipe the tears away with my hand, hoping that Tommy is right and that Shane will leave me alone from now on.

By the time we join the rest of our friends over by the bleachers, I'm starting to feel calmer. Juanita tells everyone what happened, and I can tell by the look on Tyrone's face that he's glad that I'm not going with Shane anymore. As usual, Rina has the last word. "I'm so glad you told that no-good pig to stay away from you." We all start to laugh.

That evening, while I'm sitting in the living room watching television with my mom, I decide to tell her about what happened at school with Shane. A worried look appears on her face and it stays there until I finish talking. Then, very calmly, my mom says, "I think you did the right thing, Maya."

I suddenly feel very brave. "Mom, there's something else I need to tell you about Shane," I say, pausing for a moment.

"What is it, *m'ija*?" she asks with that same worried look.

"It's kind of a long story," I answer and, suddenly, I start to tell her everything. I tell her about the night Shane and Charley showed up at the house when she was gone. I even tell her about the liquor.

When I finish, I'm sure Mom is going to scream at me or maybe tell me I'm grounded for life. But instead, she surprises me by giving me a hug and saying, "Thanks for being honest with me, *m'ija*. I always want you to feel you can trust me about anything."

I breath a sigh of relief. Maybe I won't have to lie anymore. Maybe I can just be myself. Ms. Martínez was right. I guess my mom isn't so bad after all.

NINETEEN
Ms. Martínez

I was pleased when Maya walked into my office looking bright and cheerful. As soon as she sat down, she asked me, "How was your Thanksgiving, Ms. Martínez?"

I could tell that Maya was eager to talk to me. "Oh, it was nice," I answered, trying my best to sound positive. "Frank and I went out to eat with some friends. It was the first time we've eaten at a restaurant on Thanksgiving. How was your Thanksgiving?"

"It was cool," Maya exclaimed, crossing her legs. "I went to my dad's, and you were so right about everything, Ms. Martínez. My dad and I talked a lot and he told me he's sorry for ignoring me."

"I bet that made you feel very happy."

"Yeah, it did. And he even said I shouldn't blame my mom for the divorce, that it was something that was just meant to happen. I still don't understand why it had to happen to my parents, but at least I know now that it was my dad's decision, too."

"I'm so glad you were able to talk to your dad about the divorce, Maya."

"Yeah, me too. And I even met some of my dad's new friends. I think he even has a girlfriend. Her name's Michelle."

"Oh, really?"

"Yeah, we went to eat at her apartment on Thanksgiving Day. She's sort of nice."

"And what about you and your mom? How are the two of you getting along?"

Maya uncrossed her legs and leaned back against the couch. "Pretty good. My mom's been really nice lately. We've been talking more. And you were right again, Ms. Martínez. It's not good to keep secrets. The other night I told my mom about the time when Shane and Charley forced themselves into the house. I thought she was going to have a major cow, but she was really nice about it."

It was obvious that Maya had done a lot of growing up in the past few months. "I think your mom's a very special person, too, Maya," I said, feeling pleased for Sonia as well as for myself. "And how are things going at school?"

"A lot better, Ms. Martínez. I did what you told me to do. I stood up to Shane the other day and told him that I didn't want to go with him anymore."

"That's terrific, Maya," I said, pleased that Maya was finally regaining her self-esteem and making her own decisions.

"And Shane hasn't bothered me since that day. Oh, sometimes he and Charley yell bad words at me when I walk by with Johnny, but I try to ignore them. I know Shane's jealous 'cause I'm hanging out with my old friends again."

"I think you're probably right about that, Maya. And some guys can be very persistent, but he'll get the message sooner or later."

"Yeah, that's what my mom said, too."

"Well, I'm very happy for you, Maya. It sounds like many good things are happening to you."

"Yeah, they sure are, Ms. Martínez. Everything is so much better now." Maya's face broke into a big grin, revealing those perfect white teeth that Juanita was always admiring.

"And you watch, Maya, things will keep getting better and better," I reassured her.

"And this weekend, Johnny and I are going to the mall, and then she has permission to sleep over at my house."

"That sounds like fun. Juanita has been a very good friend to you, hasn't she?"

"Yeah, I don't know what I would have done without, her."

"And I bet she doesn't know what she'd do without you," I said, glancing at my watch. "Now it looks like we're out of time, Maya. Shall we schedule another appointment?"

"Well, I was wondering if maybe I could wait until after Christmas, since it's almost vacation time and things are going so well..."

"I think that's a great idea. With Christmas right around the corner, we're all going to be very busy." I reached over and quickly flipped my desk calendar all the way past the end of December into the new year. "Why don't we see each other a week or two after Christmas? Does that sound all right to you?"

"That's cool," Maya answered, getting up from the couch.

"But remember, Maya, if you need to see me before then, just give me a call."

Maya nodded.

As I walked her out the door, Maya turned to me and said, "You know what, Ms. Martínez? I think you're pretty cool for a shrink!"

TWENTY
Ms. Martínez

As I drove home that evening, I couldn't stop thinking about Maya and how she had told me, "You were right, Ms. Martínez. It's not good to keep secrets." All of a sudden I felt myself bursting with guilt. How had I ever managed to keep my terrible secret from Frank all these years? I should have told him about it before we were married. Why couldn't I be honest, like Maya, and tell him the truth? After all, wasn't I a psychologist? Hadn't I always told my clients it was better to confront their problems? Yes. I would tell Frank tonight. I couldn't possibly go on like this much longer. I would get it over once and for all.

When I pulled into the driveway, I was surprised to see Frank's car parked in front of the house. As soon as I stepped inside the living room, Frank called out to me from the kitchen, "Hello, gorgeous. I'm in here."

I set my briefcase down on the floor and went into the kitchen to find him. Frank was standing over the stove cooking a huge pot of spaghetti sauce. This was Frank's favorite dish and the only thing he knew how to prepare. "Mmmm, smells wonderful!" I said, reaching up to kiss him.

"Not as tasty as you!" Frank replied. "I thought I'd surprise you by coming home early and cooking dinner for a change. How's the shrink business?"

"Not bad. I saw Maya today and she's feeling terrific. Everything is finally working out for her and Sonia. Let me change into my jeans and I'll come help, okay?"

I went down the hallway and into the bedroom. As I changed into some comfortable jeans and an old T-shirt, I suddenly felt nervous. How would I find the right words to tell Frank everything I needed to say to him? I sat on the bed for a few moments to try and compose my thoughts.

When I walked back into the kitchen, Frank was already setting the table. He had placed a lighted candle at the center.

"How romantic," I said, nervously.

"Sit down," Frank ordered. "Everything's ready."

While I watched Frank serve me some spaghetti, I couldn't help but think how horrified my mother would be if she could see Frank waiting on me. My mother, as well all of my aunts, was trained to believe that a good Mexican wife must wait hand and foot on her husband. Not me! It was wonderful having a husband like Frank who helped out with the cooking and the housework.

After dinner, I chased Frank into the living room then cleared the table and loaded the dishwasher. Then I joined him on the couch where he sat busily clicking the remote control from one station to the next.

I knew I couldn't stall any longer. "Frank," I interrupted. "There's something important we need to talk about."

Frank shut off the television, set the remote control down, and turned to look at me. "What is it, hon?" he asked, staring intensely at me with those sea-blue eyes that I had fallen in love with years ago.

Silence started to fill the room as I searched frantically for the right words. I wasn't quite sure how to begin.

"Sandy, what is it?" Frank asked, breaking the silence.

"It's about Raúl," I finally blurted out. "It's something I never told you. Something very painful for me."

Sensing my discomfort, Frank reached over and pulled me closer to him. "What's wrong, Sandra?" he repeated in a concerned voice.

I knew that I had Frank's full attention because he only called me Sandra when he was trying to be serious. "I don't know where to begin," I answered, pausing, and then suddenly the words all came spilling out, one after the other. I told Frank how shocked and frightened I had become when I found out I was pregnant after having separated from Raúl. I told him that I knew I couldn't go back to Raúl and continue our abusive relationship. Then I told Frank how I had agonized for weeks about what I was going to do all alone with a baby, but that when I finally miscarried, my problem was solved. Yet, all these years I had felt guilty for being relieved about losing the baby. No one had known about it—not even my own mother.

When I finally finished talking, Frank put his arms around me and held me tightly without saying a word. After a few minutes, he asked, "Sandy, why didn't you tell me?"

"I was ashamed to tell you, Frank," I answered, wiping away the tears that were running down my face. "It was something I've tried to block out all these years, erase it from my mind because it hurt so much. But when I went to Raúl's funeral, it all came back to haunt me. I'm sorry, Frank. I should have told you about it. I hope you can forgive me."

Frank caressed my face with his hand then kissed me gently on the lips. "There's nothing to forgive, Sandra. That was a long time ago and you did the best you could."

"I've wanted to tell you for so long, Frank, but I was ashamed. I didn't know what you'd think of me."

"I love you, Sandy. I always will," Frank said, kissing me again.

As we sat holding each other tightly, I knew that my own healing had just begun.

TWENTY-ONE
Maya

December is my absolute favorite month of the year. I guess that's because I was born in December and I get double presents at Christmas time. But this Christmas will be different since Dad doesn't live with us anymore. I can't help but feel sad knowing he won't be here. Mom is trying to be extra nice to me because she knows how much I miss Dad. He and I would always go pick out the Christmas tree together, but I guess this year Mom will have to take me.

One evening, Mom and I are sitting around watching a Christmas program on television when the telephone rings. Mom reaches for the receiver and after a few minutes of listening to her conversation, I realize it's Grandma calling from New Mexico. Mom's face is very tense, which makes me feel panicky. Then, all of a sudden, the strained look on Mom's face disappears and she looks more relaxed. When she finally hangs up, Mom turns to me and says, "Maya, that was your grandma. She called to tell me she's sorry about everything and wants to know if we can fly out there for Christmas. How about it? I think it's still early enough that we can get tickets. We could fly out during your school break."

My heart is pumping wildly. "Yes, Mom!" I holler. Then we both start hugging each other and jumping up and down like two crazy people. Mom is so excited that she starts looking for the suitcases while I race to my room so that I can call Juanita and tell her the good news.

The next day, Mom calls her travel agent and arranges our flights to New Mexico. We spend the next two weekends shopping for presents for Grandma and some of my relatives. It's fun going downtown with Mom because we browse around all the shops and then go to Foster Freeze to get a cone dip. I don't miss Dad as much now that I'm thinking about spending Christmas with Grandma and all my cousins.

We fly out to Santa Fe on the day before my birthday. When we deplane, Grandma and *Tía* Lola are waiting for us in the lobby. It makes me feel so happy when Mom and Grandma hug each other. Both Grandma and *Tía* Lola are crying. When Grandma finally hugs me, she tells me, "*Ay, hijita,* you're getting taller, but you're still too *flaquita.*" We all start to laugh because Grandma thinks everyone is too skinny.

That evening, Grandma's house is filled with my aunts, uncles, and cousins who have come over to eat dinner with us. I haven't seen Mom look this happy in a long time. Everyone keeps telling me how tall I am compared to my short cousins. It feels just like old times. The only thing missing is my dad.

The next morning, Dad calls to wish me a happy birthday. He tells me he's glad that Mom has patched things up with Grandma. When I ask him what he's doing on Christmas Day, he tells me he's going to spend it with some friends. I tease him and ask if he means Michelle, but he just laughs out loud. I can tell Dad is feeling happier, and that makes me feel even better. Before we hang up, Dad promises to come visit me during one of his long weekends in January.

My sixteenth birthday turns out to be one of the best birthdays I've ever had. Mom drops my cousins and me off at the movie theater and we see the new Christmas movie with Tom Hanks. It's pretty funny and we laugh a lot. When we get home, Mom orders pizza and we have a pizza birthday party. My cousins tease me because I only eat two pieces, but I tease them back that I don't want to be chubby like them. Then Grandma surprises me and brings out the birthday cake she baked for me. Everyone sings *Las mañanitas* and then I make a wish and blow out the candles. I wish that Dad is as happy as I am wherever he is. After we finish eating, I open my presents. My cousins give me a new CD, jewelry, and some new gloves. Mom gives me a new watch, and Grandma gives me some money.

On Christmas Eve, Mom and I spend the whole day helping Grandma make *tamales*. Next to Juanita's mom, Grandma makes the best *tamales* in the world. I think about Juanita and wonder if she's also helping her mom make *tamales*. By the afternoon, I am so bored with making *tamales* that

I quit, but Mom and Grandma keep at it until they finally finish.

Later in the evening, all my relatives come over to eat *tamales* with us. At midnight, we open all our presents and by the time we go to bed, it's almost three in the morning.

On Christmas Day, we go to church with Grandma and then spend the rest of the day visiting with different aunts and uncles. My cousins think I'm really cool because I'm from California, and they all beg me to spend the night at their houses. If they only knew how stuck-up a lot of people are back home, they wouldn't think California is so neat.

When the day arrives for Mom and me to go back home to Laguna, I feel sad because I know I'll miss being in Santa Fe with Grandma and all my cousins. At the airport, as Grandma hugs me tight, she reminds me to take good care of my mom for her. When we board the airplane, Mom is crying, but I can't help but feel happy that I don't have to hate Santa Fe anymore.

TWENTY-TWO
Ms. Martínez

I stared hopelessly at the dry Christmas tree, wondering whether I should take it down or leave it up until after New Year's Day. Sometimes Frank made me so angry. It never failed. Every year when we first brought the tree home, he'd be like a small child, rushing to trim it. But as soon as it came time to take it down, he disappeared.

I shrugged wearily and decided that leaving the tree up one more day wouldn't hurt. After all, I was dead tired from the holiday trips. First, we had driven to Delano and spent a few days with my parents. Then we had driven to Orange County to Frank's parents' where we spent our customary three days. And they certainly were three very long days. The smog was unbearable and my sinuses bothered me the entire time we were there. Then there was my overbearing mother-in-law. Three days were all I could stand to be around her. If it hadn't have been for Frank's older brother Bryan, I would have felt totally left out. He was the only one in Frank's family who went out of his way to make me feel comfortable. I knew that Bryan sincerely liked and appreciated this "Mexican."

The sound of the doorbell interrupted my thoughts. I slipped my shoes back on and lifted my tired body off the couch. When I opened the front door, I was happy to see Maya and Juanita.

"What a nice surprise," I said. "Come on in."

"*Feliz Navidad,* Ms. Martínez," Juanita said as she and Maya stepped into the living room.

As I motioned for them to sit down, I smiled to myself. Maya was wearing purple stretch pants that made her look skinnier than a bean pole.

"We wanted to surprise you," Maya said.

Then Juanita handed me a brown paper bag. "My *Amá* sent you these *tamales*. She also sent some hot chile 'cause she remembered how much your husband likes her chile."

"That was so nice of her," I answered, setting the bag down on the coffee table. "Frank is going to go crazy with your mom's chile. He says I never make it hot enough."

"How was your Christmas, Ms. Martínez?" Maya asked me.

"Oh, it was very nice. We went to my parents' house and then over to Frank's in Orange County."

"What did *Santa Clos* bring you, Ms. Martínez?" Juanita asked.

"Oh, the usual: perfume, clothes. Frank gave me a sexy black leather skirt."

"*¡Híjole!*" Juanita said, and we all started laughing.

"This is for you, Ms. Martínez," Maya said, reaching over and handing me a beautifully wrapped package. "I bought it in Santa Fe. My mom and I flew there for Christmas and we had the best time ever. Mom and Grandma made up."

Maya's eyes were shining and I could tell she was bursting with joy. "That's wonderful, Maya," I told her. "I am so happy for both you and your mom. But you didn't have to bring me anything."

"I wanted to thank you for helping me."

"Open it, Ms. Martínez," Juanita ordered.

"I love opening presents!" I said as I began to peel off the bright wrapping paper. When I removed the cover from the box, I found a delicate hand-carved wooden figure inside. "It's beautiful, Maya," I sighed, carefully taking it out of the box and setting it on the table next to me.

"It's a Kachina doll, Ms. Martínez," Maya proudly explained. "It's a holy spirit that is supposed to protect you."

"I love Native American art. Thank you so much, Maya," I said, reaching over to hug her. Then I turned to look at Juanita. "Now, how about having a soda with me?"

"Sorry, Ms. Martínez," Juanita answered. "We have to go. We're going over to the mall."

"Can I give you a ride?"

"No, thanks, Ms. Martínez," Maya said. "We're taking the bus over to Ankiza's house and then her mom is dropping us off at the mall."

"Are you meeting anyone special over there?" I asked mischieviously.

Maya and Juanita glanced at each other and started giggling.

"I see," I said, laughing out loud.

"Well, we better go," Maya said, standing up.

I followed them to the door and gave them each a big hug. As I closed the door behind me, I couldn't help but feel a deep sense of satisfaction. Frank was right. This was why I had become a professional: to feel good by helping people. And that was all that really mattered.

Glossary

Amá—mother

Apá—father—

Ay, hijita—Oh, dear daughter

Antonio Aguilar—one of Mexico's most celebrated balladeers and film stars

Aztlán—Náhuatl term used by the Aztecs as the name of their original homeland, which many scholars believe was located in the American Southwest

barrio—an Hispanic neighborhood

Cállate!—Shut up!

César Chávez—an important Chicano leader/activist who founded the United Farm Workers Union

chaparra—shorty

Chicano (a)—a person of Mexican descent raised in the U.S.

Chicanos—plural form of Chicano/a

chile jalapeño—jalapeño pepper

cholo (a)—contemporary Chicano youth who dress distinctively and rebel against mainstream culture

¡Cómo que no!—But of course!

comadre—godmother, protector, friend, comrade

comadres—plural form of comadre

compadre—godfather, protector, friend, comrade
compañeras (os)—companions

Dolores Huerta—important Chicana leader/ activist; co-founder of the United Farm Workers Union
dinero—money

ese—slang word used as a greeting which means "homeboy"
esa—slang word used as a greeting which means "homegirl"
¿Estás loca?—Are you crazy?

Feliz Navidad—Merry Christmas
Flaca—skinny

gringos—Anglo-Americans

hija—daughter
¡Híjole!—Wow! My goodness! Oh my gosh!

José Montoya—Chicano poet/painter; founder of the RCAF or Royal Chicano Air Force, a collective of Chicano painters based in Sacramento, California.

Las Mañanitas—traditional Mexican song that is played for someone's birthday
Llegaste temprano—You arrived early
Los Lobos—popular Chicano Rock group from East L.A.
Madre de Dios, hija—For God's sake, daughter
m'ija—the contraction of "my daughter"

mocosas—snot-nosed girls; sometimes used endearingly
mocosos—snot-nosed boys

¡Orale!—Hey! Okay! Right on! All right!

Pachuco talk—refers to the dialect Caló or the speech style of Pachucos and Cholos, that is a mixture of Spanish and English
panza—belly

Qué flaca estás, hija—You're so skinny, daughter
Qué viva—Long live, hail

Raza—Race, lineage, family; La Raza includes all Latinos regardless of nationality; literally, "the race of people"

Santa Clos—Santa Claus
¡sinvergüenza!—a shameless person

tía—aunt

Unión de Campesinos—United Farm Workers Union

¡Vámonos!—Let's go!
Virgin of Guadalupe—Mexico's most honored patron saint, the brown Virgin Mary